𝕳.𝕬.𝕱.𝕹.𝕿.𝕾

All through the city and its suburbs, the past lies behind the present and ghosts shadow the living. There are threshold zones, borderlines, and places where the laws of time and space falter. Strange things can happen, the barriers between the worlds grow thin and it is possible, just possible, to move from one world to another . . .

Prepare to enter 𝕳.𝕬.𝕱.𝕹.𝕿.𝕾 – a strange terrifying world with forces of good and evil. Evil so deadly that even the *ghosts* fear for their lives . . .

The 𝕳.𝖆.𝖀.𝕹.𝕿.𝕾 *Series*

H·A·U·N·T·S

S is for SHUDDER

CELIA REES

Hodder
Children's
Books

A division of Hodder Headline plc

Copyright © 1998 Celia Rees

First published in Great Britain in 1998
by Hodder Children's Books

The right of Celia Rees to be identified as the Author of the
Work has been asserted by her in accordance with the
Copyright, Designs and Patents Act 1988.

10 9 8 7 6 5 4 3 2 1

A Catalogue record for this book
is available from the British Library

ISBN 0340 71527 8

Typeset by Hewer Text Ltd, Edinburgh
Printed and bound in Great Britain

Hodder Children's Books
A Division of Hodder Headline plc
338 Euston Road
London NW1 3BH

Contents

Come away, O human child!
To the waters and the wild
With a faery, hand in hand,
For the world's more full of weeping than
you can understand.

W.B. Yeats 'The Stolen Child'

And if any gaze on our rushing band,
We come between him and the deed of his hand,
We come between him and the hope of his heart.

W.B. Yeats 'The Hosting of the Sidhe'

1

Distant Laughter

'Kate, Kate!'

Kate Williams turned, surprised to hear her name being called. She pushed her fair hair back from her damp forehead and squinted into the bright sunlight, peering through the end of day crowd jostling out of the school gates. She was even more surprised to see Lisa Wilson, one of her brother's friends, jump off the fence and come running towards her. Although their schools were on the same site, Kate was fourteen and went to a different part to Davey. The Senior School had a different finishing time, so Lisa must have been there for at least twenty minutes.

'Can I have a word with you?'

'Yes, sure,' Kate stood, bag balanced on hip, waiting for the younger girl. It was a hot day in the middle of June and her summer uniform shirt was sticking to her back. The sun had been beating against the glass windows of her classroom all afternoon, but it wasn't much cooler outside.

'What's up?' She asked as Lisa joined her.

'It's about Davey,' the other girl replied, but would say no more until they were through the throng waiting for buses and lifts.

'What about him?' Kate asked as they took the path that led across to Derry Hollow and up to the Puckeridge Estate where they both lived.

Lisa hung back, making sure there was a good wide space between them and the little knot of girls walking along in front of them. She looked round before she spoke, to see that there was no one coming up behind them. It was clear that whatever she wanted to speak about was private.

'It's about Davey . . .'

'You said that already. Look, Lisa . . .'

Kate looked down at the other girl, thinking that she knew where this might be heading. Lisa and Davey were good friends, close friends. They saw each other all the time. They sat next to each other in class. Relationships started young these days. When she was in Year Seven, loads in her class had been going out with each other. Kate could sympathise, but she did not want to act as some kind of Agony Aunt sorting out her younger brother's love life.

'I don't know how it is with you two,' she went on, 'and frankly I'm not sure I want to, but, well, maybe he's a little too young. Boys mature later than girls . . .'

'What are you talking about?' Lisa looked up at Kate, her grey eyes puzzled, black brows drawn together in a frown. 'Oh, no,' she added, colouring as she realised what Kate was getting at. 'Oh, no,' she repeated, shaking her head for emphasis. 'It's not that. It's *nothing* like that!'

'Oh, right.' It was Kate's turn to blush at her own misunderstanding. 'What is it then?'

'He's been acting strangely, that's all.'

'In what way?'

'Well,' Lisa frowned again, trying to think how to describe it. 'He's kind of not there half the time, like he's on a different planet . . .'

'So?' Kate grinned. 'What's new?'

Lisa shook her short dark curls. 'This isn't the same. He just doesn't seem interested in anything. Like – we started this project together at the beginning of term – about The Crusades – and he was all fired up about it to start with – got loads of books did lots of work, but just lately he's done nothing, left it all up to me.'

'Well, that's the problem with projects . . .' Kate said vaguely. She didn't want to get involved in petty work squabbles, either. She wasn't her brother's teacher.

'Don't get me wrong,' Lisa corrected her. 'I don't *mind* doing it, it's just, it's just not like him. We've done tons of projects together and he never shirks his part of the work. It's like something's turned off inside him. He's just not interested in anything. He goes off on his own, like at lunch and breaktime, and he never calls for me, you know, to walk to school, and he's out as soon as the bell goes. It's not just me,' she added quickly, in case Kate began to get the wrong idea again, 'he's avoiding everybody. I mean, he's never hung round with a gang, but he's not a loner, he's always been sociable, up for a game of football and that, but now he never joins in anything. Haven't you noticed?'

'Well . . .' Kate stopped for a moment to consider whether to tell Lisa what was essentially Davey's business, 'yes,' she said eventually. 'He's been behaving the same way at home. He's been losing weight, too. Don't say I told you, but Mum's even taken him to the doctor to find out what's wrong with him.'

'What did the doctor say?'

'Nothing,' Kate shrugged. 'Couldn't find anything. Gran puts it down to "out-growing his strength" and says he needs a tonic. Mum's been muttering about "growth spurts" and hormones and dosing him with vitamins.'

4

'He has been getting thinner,' Lisa agreed. 'Maybe that's why he looks different.'

'How do you mean, different?'

They were coming out of the entry where the path came into Derry Hollow. From here, their homes lay in different directions. Lisa lived in Garden Court, a block of maisonettes off to the left up Puckeridge Rise. Kate's house was on Derry Way, which led up to the right. They stopped in front of the wide drive leading down to Derry House. The tall Victorian house at the bottom of the estate had been empty for some time. It was still creepy, despite the fact that someone had finally bought it and builders' vans stood around on the buckled tarmac. The windows were boarded and plastered with signs; blue plastic shutes snaked down from the roof to a series of skips. But, even on a day like this, the house seemed all in shadow, the air around it chilly. Kate rubbed her arms. It was definitely what Mrs Craggs would call a 'cold spot'. Kate shuddered. She did not like to linger here, despite the hot brightness of the day. She still had nightmares about what had happened in there at Hallowe'en. First to Davey, and then their confrontation with The Lady. She had a feeling that whoever bought it, and whatever they did to it, the building would always belong to her, it

5

would never lose its brooding atmosphere of ancient malice.

'Well,' Lisa was saying, 'his face looks thinner, especially since he had that haircut—'

'Pardon?' Kate had been so lost in thought that she had forgotten what they were talking about, or even that Lisa was with her.

'Davey. You asked how he looked different.'

'Oh, yeah, right. I'll check on him. Don't worry . . .'

Kate suddenly seemed in a hurry to go.

'That's not the only thing.' Lisa caught her arm. 'It's his eyes—'

'His eyes?' Kate stopped and looked down at the other girl. 'What about them?'

'I could be imagining it . . .' Lisa started, knowing how strange this was going to sound, 'but they seem to be going a different colour.'

'A different colour? What on earth do you mean?'

'I don't know, exactly,' the younger girl shrugged. 'It's, it's hard to explain . . .' She thought about Davey's distinctive dark brown eyes. 'They seem to be getting lighter.'

Kate frowned, bringing her brother's face to mind. There did seem something odd about it. Weight loss and a new haircut could certainly account for his changing appearance – but his *eyes*?

'You have to be mistaken, Lisa.' She shook her head, not really wanting to acknowledge what the girl had said. 'People's eyes do not change colour.'

Kate's voice sounded loud, echoing off the houses on the quiet estate. In the silence of the hot afternoon it seemed to be followed by another sound. A high silvery chuckle. Kate looked round. The hair was like fur on her arms now. The laugh was coming from the Hollow. It could be a radio, or one of the workmen, but it sounded light, like a woman's voice, and it didn't sound human. Kate had heard the high ringing tone before, in the basement of Derry House.

2

Behaving Strangely

When Kate got in, Davey was sitting at the kitchen table flicking over the pages of a magazine. He barely looked up as his sister entered the room, but that wasn't unusual. They quite often ignored each other as they went about the routines of family life. Kate got herself a drink and something to eat and sat down opposite him.

'Mum in yet?'

'No.'

'How about Emma?'

'Upstairs.'

'What are you going to do tonight?'

'What's it to you?' Davey held his football magazine up higher.

'Just wondered if there was anything good on the telly.'

'How should I know?' Davey concentrated his attention on an item at the bottom of the page. 'Go and get the TV guide.'

Kate went and fetched it out of the living-room.

'Just repeats,' she said as she studied the page. 'Maybe we could get a video. There are a couple of new ones out. We could go down the video shop and have a look, get some coke and pop-corn—'

'You do what you like,' Davey cut her short. He folded his magazine and stood up. 'I've got things to do.'

'Oh,' Kate's voice remained level. She didn't want to show how his abrupt rejection had stung. 'Like what?'

'Homework. I've got a project to finish.'

He left the room without a backward glance. There was no chance to check on the colour of his eyes. He hadn't even looked at her.

Kate went upstairs. Davey's door was firmly closed. She thought about knocking, but went on past. He might get suspicious if she paid too much attention and she didn't want to spook him, or get Lisa into trouble. She went into her own room and lay on the bed, trying to think of a different approach. After a moment or two, there was a small knock on the door.

'Come in!'

'It's me,' Emma, Kate's younger sister, came into

the room. 'I want someone to listen to my reading. I asked Davey, but he told me not to bother him; said that he was busy . . .'

Emma hung back by the door, not wanting to invite another refusal.

'Come on in,' Kate smiled, 'I'll have a listen.'

Kate patted the bed next to her. Emma extracted her reading book from the battered ziplock bag that she had been hiding behind her back and came to sit by her sister. She flattened the book out on her knees, holding it open at the right place. Her recently cut chin-length bob fell forward, shading her face. She read using her special, careful 'reading book' voice, pointing each word out with a stubby finger and beating out the rhythm with her heels. Emma was eight, but tall for her age. Her long legs were brown from wearing shorts all the time, and scabbed and scratched from playground falls.

Kate looked up and caught a glimpse of them both, side by side, in the mirror. They were like each other in looks: the same slim build, silky fair hair and cornflower-blue eyes. It was the kind of similarity constantly remarked upon by relatives, teachers, friends of the family. Davey had always been the odd one out; as compact and dark as they were willowy and fair. He didn't really look much like Mum, or Dad either, for that matter. 'Where did he spring from?' people would joke. As though he didn't fit with the rest of them. As though he'd been swopped at birth — like a changeling . . .

'You're not listening,' Emma complained.

'Yes, I am.'

'What's it about then?'

Kate took a quick squint at the cover. 'It's about a little boy who's lost his dog.'

It wasn't entirely a wild guess. A lot of Emma's books seemed to involve children who mislaid their pets.

'Hmm,' Emma was still suspicious. 'Where does he find it?'

'I don't know,' Kate shrugged her shoulders. 'We haven't got to that bit yet.'

'All right.' Emma seemed satisfied with that answer. She grinned, her new front teeth looked too big in her elfin face. 'I'll read some more, then. We are supposed to do at least as far as the next bit or Mrs Thompson gets cross.'

'Yeah, sure. Read to the end if you like.'

'Oh, no,' Emma shook her head, serious again. 'You mustn't do that. She gets cross if you do that, too.'

'Whatever,' Kate leaned back. 'Do as much as you want, and then I want to ask you something.'

'What did you want to ask me?'

'What?' Kate had been lying back on the bed, almost asleep, lulled by her sister's reading.

'I've finished my reading,' Emma explained patiently. 'You said you wanted to ask me something.'

'Oh, right,' Kate struggled up. 'It was about Davey.'

'What about him?'

'Have you noticed anything . . .' Kate thought for a moment, wondering how to put this, '. . . well . . . odd about him lately.'

'No,' Emma shook her head. 'He hasn't been horrible, if that's what you mean.'

Emma was nearer to Davey in age. The two of them tended to squabble and fight much more with each other than they did with Kate.

'You mean he's being nice?'

'Not exactly. He just ignores me,' Emma stopped to think. 'No, it's more than that. He lets me watch what I want on TV, he even lets me play with his things. It's like he can't be bothered. There's something else . . .' Emma looked at her sister, wondering whether to say.

12

'What?' Kate hugged her knees.

'Well, it's at night . . . I hear him sometimes.'

'Hear what? His stereo?'

Emma's room and Davey's were separated only by a thin partition. He'd been told off before for disturbing her.

'No,' Emma shook her head again. 'I hardly ever hear that. I didn't think he played it any more. It's, well, I hear noises . . .'

'What kind of noises?'

'First off, I thought it was ghosts, like in the dream I had at Hallowe'en. Oh, I know I was silly and they weren't real,' she added quickly, misinterpreting the concern on Kate's face. 'And I don't believe in them any more, not really, but when I heard the noises, I thought of them.'

'But it wasn't them?' Kate asked weakly.

The ghosts at Hallowe'en had been real enough, but Kate thought that Emma had forgotten the hideous clown and his ghastly crew. She thought that Emma accepted that they were just figures from a nightmare. Now she was forced to wonder exactly how much her sister did remember.

'How could it be? They don't exist!' Emma said, to Kate's relief. 'Sometimes you are silly, Katie!' she added with a grin. Her new teeth gave her a slight lisp. 'No,' her bobbed hair swung out and back again, 'it was Davey.'

'What was he doing?'

'Getting up and padding about, in his room and around the house.'

'That's not so unusual,' Kate said. 'It has been very hot. Perhaps he couldn't sleep and went downstairs to get a drink, or something.'

'Perhaps,' Emma nodded. 'But he didn't come upstairs with anything in his hands. One night I got up my courage to peep out. I'd heard him go downstairs, so I looked over the banisters.'

'What was he doing?'

'He was in the hall. Then he went to the front door.' Emma walked her fingers over the duvet cover. 'Really really quietly. I thought he was trying to let someone in,' she shivered, unable to stop herself thinking about the ghosts, despite telling Kate she didn't believe in them. 'But I don't think he was trying to do that.'

'What was he trying to do, then?'

'I think he was trying to get out. He couldn't, because of the new lock Dad put on, but what I want to know is . . .' she turned to Kate, her head held on one side like a curious bird, 'why would he want to go out in his pyjamas at two o'clock in the morning?'

'I don't know, Em. I really don't.'

Kate leaned over and gave her little sister a hug. It was not until that moment that she realised just how much she missed Davey, just how far he had withdrawn from the family.

3

Night Walkers

Davey hardly emerged from his room these days – except to eat. At her next opportunity Kate tried to get a good look at him, to see if Lisa was right about his eyes, but she failed. He didn't look up from his plate. When he had finished, he was back up the stairs, using the project as his reason for leaving them. Mum didn't say anything as he excused himself, but Kate could not fail to miss the look her parents exchanged as he left the kitchen.

'Sort out your room while you're up there,' Mum called up the stairs. 'Tom and Ellie are coming for the weekend, so make sure it's tidy.'

'It already is,' Davey shouted back from the landing.

His dad raised an eyebrow, but his Mum nodded to confirm that it was true. His sudden tidiness was another worrying sign. Davey's room had been a tip since he was a toddler. They had tried threats and bribes, but nothing worked. Even when Mum had gone in, armed with bin bags and the Hoover to give

16

it a thorough going-over, all the junk just reappeared as if from nowhere, along with the other mess.

No light showed under Davey's door when Kate went to bed. She paused for a second, hand up, ready to knock, but thought better of it. Perhaps he was asleep, and even if he wasn't, what would she say? She thought of the evidence she had accumulated and turned away. You could hardly burst into someone's room and start accusing them of acting strangely, just because they were not talking much and had begun to keep their room tidy.

Kate went into her own room instead and got ready for bed. She lay down with no intention of sleeping. Davey was the one who had premonitions, 'feelings'. He had the 'sight', he knew when things were going to happen, but Kate had her own intuitions. Nothing to do with the supernatural, these were to do with ordinary life and real people. She lay in the dark reviewing the concerns expressed about Davey: by Lisa, her parents, herself and Emma. Taken on their own, they did not add up to very much, but taken together . . .

Kate woke with a start. She must have fallen asleep, despite intending to stay awake. She glanced at the clock radio by her bed. The digital display said: 2:03. She leaned up on one elbow, trying to recall what had woken her up, when she heard it again. A faint pattering, followed by an indistinct shuffling . . .

Kate's heart beat fast and she felt the hairs rising up on her bare arms. Like Emma, she was reminded of the white-faced clown, with his sunken liquid eyes, and little yellow teeth sharp inside the wide red grinning mouth. What if he had come back again? What if he had his hideous comrades with him: the black-draped skeleton and the rubber-faced klansman? There was no reason why it shouldn't happen. Stranger things had, Kate knew for a fact. The clown had got in to the house at Hallowe'en, so why not now? Dad had fitted new locks, but locks and bolts would not bar their way. They were not human.

She looked around the room, eyes wide, alert to any small changes. Sure enough, there was a big bulky shape by the door. That had not been there before. The door was partially opened. It must have slipped in and now she couldn't get out. It was between her and the only exit. Kate kept quite still, her eyes trained on it, ready to detect any little movement. As she watched, it began to sway slightly, as if suddenly aware of her, perhaps alerted by her attention. It was gathering strength, slowly readying itself to come and get her.

It seemed in no hurry. Kate stayed frozen, still balanced on one elbow, half-rising, half-lying, while her heart hammered painfully in her chest and fresh sweat broke out all over. The 'thing' kept up its slow swaying motion, but didn't move any further. Kate forced herself to focus on it and take a good look. It was man-height and wearing a coat, with broad straight shoulders, but no hands. Where the head should be was a little round hook . . .

Kate fell back on the bed, not sure whether to laugh or cry, as relief flooded through her. It was her blazer. The breeze from the open window was causing it to swing about like that. Mum must have collected it from the cleaners and put it on a hanger behind the door. Kate hadn't noticed.

Kate looked at the ceiling, to where twin lights were zipping about. She grinned to herself. Not UFOs, or anything like that. These were old friends. Car headlights climbing the hill.

Just when you think you're safe . . .

Kate sat up again.

There was something moving in the mirror. Her heartbeat instantly returned to its former rapid rate. She had to bite the side of her mouth to stop herself from screaming out. She remembered the mirror in the Room of Ceremonies; it acted as a portal between this world and another. Now, here in her own mirror, in her own room, a ghostly figure was stealing towards her . . .

4

Doppelgänger

'It's only me.'

Emma turned to the bed, surprised to see her sister with the duvet clutched up to her neck, her eyes seeming black, wide and terrified, her face white in the moonlight seeping in through a gap in the curtains.

'Who did you think it was?'

'I–I don't know . . .' Kate reached across and pretended to look at the clock, not wanting Emma to see how frightened she was. 'What are you doing in here anyway?' she whispered fiercely. 'It's two o'clock in the morning!'

'I heard Davey get up. I just came to tell you . . .'

Emma hovered uncertainly. Kate had failed to hide her fear. Emma was astonished, and not a little shocked, to find that her big sister could be scared – just like her.

'Where is he now?' Kate scrambled out of bed.

'I–I don't know . . . downstairs I think.' She hesitated. 'You aren't angry with me?'

'No,' Kate managed a smile and ruffled her sister's hair. 'It's just you gave me a bit of a fright. You shouldn't go creeping round people's rooms in the middle of the night.'

'I just wanted you to know about Davey. And I had to be quiet, in case Mum or Dad heard me.'

'Okay, okay. You go back to bed now. I'll go and see what he's up to.'

Kate took Emma back along the landing and then sneaked a look into her brother's room. She could see Davey plainly. His body humped up under the duvet, his dark head resting on the pillow. His face was turned away from her, but he seemed fast asleep. He was not restless in any way and his breathing was deep and regular. Either he had been there all the time, or he had gone back to bed. Kate withdrew quietly, her feelings torn between annoyance and relief. Whichever way, Emma had got her up for nothing.

She stood for a moment, looking over the banister. The stairs were bathed in moonlight, below them was a deep well of shadow. Nothing stirred. Everything was quiet except for the ticking of the hall clock. There was no movement at all, but suddenly her earlier fears came flooding back. Coats huddled round the hat stand like ghosts conspiring, and every gleam of light seemed like eyes looking up at her. The blackness through the glass front door appeared solid, as if the Sentinels were massing . . .

Kate wiped the beads of sweat from her upper lip. She had to get a grip. She was getting worse than Emma. There was nothing down there, she told herself. Nothing! She turned away, getting ready to go back to her own room when a sudden slight shift caught her attention.

There *was* something down there . . .

What she saw scared her far more than any leering white-faced clown or black-robed Sentinel. She drew back instinctively, melting into the shadows, as a figure came gliding into view and began climbing, ascending the stairs on silent feet. It was her brother. But how could that be? Kate put her hand to her mouth to stop herself from crying out. She glanced over to Davey's half-open bedroom door. His form was still under the bed clothes. And yet . . . and yet . . . The figure advanced, walking up the stairs, coming towards her. It was him, but not him. It was his fetch, co-walker, double, *doppelgänger*. The ghostly embodiment of a living human being.

Kate drew back from the banister. Instinct told her not to let it see her. It was like him, but not like. The same height, same size, same clothes, but the face looked narrower, the cheekbones higher. His skin looked white, almost transparent. His short hair stood up like fur over his head. His ears seemed more pointed, set at an odd angle. And his eyes . . .

His eyes were open wide and, in the moonlight streaming down from the window above, they seemed to shine a pale golden amber.

Kate didn't wait to see what happened when the thing went into Davey's room. She crept back to her bed badly frightened, thoroughly spooked. She pulled the duvet round her and then up over her head, blotting out the metallic shafts of moonlight that were coating the room in a weird, unearthly light. She curled herself up in a little ball, her eyes shut tight. She didn't want to see anything else, she just wanted to be inside a cocoon of absolute darkness. Even though the night was still hot, she could not stop shivering and her teeth would not stop chattering.

What was happening to Davey? Kate could not even guess, but one thing she did know – she couldn't handle it on her own. She let up a silent prayer of thanks that Tom and Elinor were coming this weekend. Their visit coincided with the summer solstice. Midsummer. A year to the day since they had gone on the Haunts Ghost Tour and stumbled into the ghost city and this whole thing had started. They planned to go again, this time to say 'goodbye'. The ghosts were leaving the city, and it would be forever.

Kate hoped that they had not already gone. She badly needed help and there was nobody else. Somehow she knew that no one from her world could save Davey now, not even the medium, Mrs Sylvia Craggs.

Time crept on towards morning and gradually Kate relaxed and went to sleep. In her dreams, she journeyed through deserted city streets, setting out to search for the Blind Fiddler, and the highwayman, Jack Cade, and the others in his ghost crew: Elizabeth, Polly and Govan. She had to find them. Only ghosts would know what was wrong with Davey and how to save him.

5

Hag-ridden

'What's the matter with you two?' Alison Williams asked when Kate and Davey came down for breakfast. 'You look hag-ridden, the both of you.'

'What does that mean?' Emma asked. 'They've been giving old ladies piggybacks?'

'Something like that,' her mother laughed. 'It's just an expression. It means when you wake up tired for no reason.'

'I didn't sleep very well,' Kate supplied. 'It was too hot.'

'What about you, Davey?' Emma looked over to her brother.

'I slept okay,' he answered, although there were dark smudges under his eyes.

'But you can't stop yawning!'

'Stop bugging me, will you?' He turned on his sister. 'I told you, I slept okay.'

'Wait up, Davey,' Kate said when they were ready to go to school. 'I'll walk with you.'

She was hoping to talk to him, perhaps find out what was wrong with him, but he was halfway out of the door.

'Can't stop,' he shouted over his shoulder. 'I'm meeting Lisa.'

He'd grabbed his bag and was off down the path before Kate could stop him. She went to school with Emma instead. As they walked down the road, Kate mentioned casually about Emma coming to her room, but her sister didn't seem to remember a thing about it. All Kate got was a puzzled look before Emma ran on ahead to meet her friends. Kate let her go. She did not want to alarm her by questioning too closely, and she really was tired, her head full of images from her troubled night. She was having a problem working out what was dream and what was reality. Had she really seen Davey in two places at once? It seemed less and less likely. It seemed like a dream now, like the one where she was searching endlessly, looking for phantoms in the dark moonless streets of a ghost city.

The sunlit suburban road was busy, full of women with buggies, kids going to school, cars pulling out to go to work. Kate drifting along, weaving a way through them all, lost in thought. Suddenly Emma was back by her side, tugging at her bag.

'What is it? What's the matter?' Kate looked down at her sister

'It's Lisa.'

Kate looked up. 'What about her?'

'Davey said he was going to meet her, but she's there on her own.'

Emma pointed to a small, dark, curly-haired figure, dressed in a white polo shirt and khaki shorts, coming down Puckeridge Rise. Kate sent Emma on ahead, but she waited where the roads met. She wanted a word with Lisa.

'I think you're right,' she said, when the younger girl came up. 'I think there *is* something wrong with him.'

'Any idea what?' Lisa asked as they made their way along the path that led round Derry Hollow and towards the school.

'No,' Kate shook her head. She had decided not to tell Lisa about the *other* Davey since she was no longer sure that she'd seen him herself. If Emma could not remember coming into her room, it meant that she could have dreamt the whole thing. 'But do me a favour,' she added. 'Keep an eye on him at school and report anything strange, anything at all.'

'Sure.'

'Ellie and Tom are coming at the weekend,' Kate

added. 'Perhaps Davey'll talk to Tom. Maybe it's a boy thing.'

'Umm, could be,' Lisa nodded, but she did not look completely convinced.

They were nearly at the gates now. Kate looked at her watch. Her school day started before Lisa's did. The Senior bell was about to go any minute.

'I've got to go,' she said. 'I'll meet you here, say quarter to four? See if there's anything more to report. We should be able to get to the bottom of it.'

'I hope so . . .'

'I reckon we can. If we all work together,' Kate said with a smile, trying to reassure herself as well as Lisa.

Lisa sat next to Davey, watching but not watching, keeping an eye out for any strange behaviour, anything she could tell Kate about, but there was nothing. That was the trouble. It wasn't what he was doing, she considered, it was what he wasn't – that's where the strangeness lay. He stared out of the window a lot, but who didn't? On a hot day like this, even their teacher, Mr Craddock, gazed long-ingly outside, probably dreaming about doing his garden.

When he wasn't looking out of the window,

Davey got on with his work. He did nothing to draw attention to himself. He spoke when spoken to. He answered questions, but he joined in none of the chatter and banter that went on when Craddock wasn't looking, or was inclined to let up a bit. Davey was not a swot, or a creep, by any means. He was normally up for most things, but now it was as if he was on autopilot. At break and lunchtime he mooched round by himself. He seemed to sleepwalk through the day.

Davey and Lisa were good friends, best friends in many ways. They had been through a lot together, like that episode at Christmas, with Miss Malkin and the Victorian ghost girl, Elizabeth Hamilton. What had occurred then had been terrifying, but so weird that Lisa sometimes thought that it had not happened at all. They had somehow slipped through time into a different period in the history of the city. They had got caught up in an air raid. Lisa had met her own great-grandfather. They had never discussed what happened, but the strange events had made them even closer.

What he was like now . . . Lisa toyed with her pen, doodling on her rough book. There was a time in the Peace Garden, when it was all over . . . What he was like now reminded her a bit of what he was like then. He had been dazed, stunned by something only he could see and hear. The world around seemed to fade to him; he seemed to be in a different one to her. There was someone he called 'The Lady', someone Miss Malkin was supposed to be. When he spoke of her, his eyes went wide and distant, kind of like they were now.

Lisa risked a sideways look at him. That might account for his expression, but not the change of colour. His deep brown eyes were getting lighter, with a reddish shine in them, almost as if he was wearing colour contact lenses . . .

'What are you staring at?' Davey looked up suddenly, giving her the full benefit of his amber glare.

'You.'

'Well, don't.'

'I just wondered if you were okay.'

'Of course I am.' Davey snapped. 'Why shouldn't I be? Do me a favour, Lisa.' Davey turned his chair so his back was to her. 'Leave me alone.'

Across the table, Billy Hawking went 'ooo-ooh' and pulled his face into a horrible simper before nudging his neighbour and saying 'lover's tiff' in an exaggerated whisper. Lisa ignored him and got on with her work. When the bell went for the end of the day, Davey stood up from the table and left without saying a word.

'Nothing to report, I'm afraid,' she said when she met Kate.

'Never mind,' Kate shrugged, but she looked disappointed.

'Just one thing . . .'

As they walked along, Lisa explained her theory about Davey and The Lady.

'Does that make any sense?' she asked when she had finished.

'Yes,' Kate replied, sounding a little bit brighter. 'Yes, it just might. Thanks, Lisa.'

'No problem,' Lisa looked up at the older girl and then away again. 'Davey means a lot to me,' she blushed slightly. 'I don't mean in *that* way. I just mean he's a really good friend. I don't know what's wrong with him, but if I can help in any way at all . . .'

'Yeah, I know.'

'He'd do the same for me, if he was acting normal. That's what's odd – he's usually really caring and loyal – and funny,' Lisa paused for a moment. 'I can't remember the last time he cracked a joke, or even smiled.'

'Hmm, that's true.'

Kate couldn't recall the last time herself, come to think of it. Must have been back in May. After they had helped the ghosts to defeat Eugene Hutton, the ghost-hunter. The last time the twins were here. She remembered Davey having a laugh with them. It was round about her birthday. They had gone to the Mayday Fair as part of the celebrations. She remembered Tom and Davey had been joking about something on the way there.

'It's little things,' Lisa was saying. 'Today at dinner, for instance. The helpers like Davey – I mean, he's *usually* so cheery. We had semolina. They know he likes it, he's about the only person who does, so they give him more, with an extra dollop of jam as well. Today he didn't even say "thank you", and he hardly touched it. It's only a small thing.' She made a sign with finger and thumb. 'But small things mount up.' She half-turned away, and when she went on her voice was quiet. 'It's as though he doesn't care about anything any more.'

'I know what you mean.' Kate had been thinking the same thing. 'But maybe it's just us. Maybe he needs to see different faces. Tom and Ellie are coming. We plan to go into town tomorrow night.'

'That's a good idea. Take him out of himself a bit.'

'Yeah,' Kate nodded, 'that's what I thought.'

'Well,' Lisa turned to go. 'I hope it works. See you, Kate.'

'Yeah. See you, Lisa.'

Kate watched the younger girl go. Tomorrow night, she intended to go on another ghost walk. Not one run by Haunts Tours, one of her own devising. It was a long-standing arrangement. The ghosts were leaving the city, and this would be their last chance to see them. Now the ghost walk had added importance. Kate didn't know, any more than Lisa, what was the matter with her brother, but the feeling she had was growing stronger: only the ghosts could help him now.

6

Kate's Dream

Kate's disturbed sleep from the night before caught up with her and that night she went to bed early. The heat of the day still lingered and light from outside peeped through her curtains, but she went to sleep easily enough.

At first her sleep was deep and dreamless, but gradually she began to surface into a world so real that she could not be completely sure whether she was dreaming or not. She was in the ghost city, just as she had been the night before, and she was searching, looking for somebody, or something, but she did not know what. Maybe she was looking for Davey. Maybe she was looking for someone to help him . . .

She set off down narrow twisting streets, past deserted higgledy-piggledy timber-framed houses louring down at her from under a dull grey-brownish sky. It was not like the times she had been there before. What Kate saw made her increasingly uneasy. The Judge's house, in Fiddler's Court, looked burnt out. The doors and windows were empty spaces, sooty black scorch marks licked up from the shattered casements, staining the grey stone.

All the houses seemed empty. On Quarry Street doors were hanging open. Johnswell's cobbles were littered with torn items of clothing, battered pots and pans, broken crockery. Her uneasiness was rapidly turning into a creeping fear. Jack Cade had said that the ghosts were leaving, but this looked liked a city that had suffered sacking and looting after the population had fled.

She turned the last corner, making for *The Seven Dials*, the inn where Jack Cade and his ghost crew lived. He had told her that they were not leaving until midsummer, and it was not midsummer yet. She stood outside the large timber-framed building. It told that same story. Doors open, windows smashed. The inn sign was hanging off its hinges. It looked like someone had used it for target practice.

Kate turned away in bitter disappointment. There was obviously no one there to help her. She reached Harrow Lane, the old thoroughfare leading out of the city. It was as empty of life as a sepia print. Kate looked up and down, her frustration blooming into panic. If the ghosts had left then who, or what, remained here?

As if on cue, she had a sudden strong feeling of being watched. She looked around, even more fearful. She set off again, starting down the steep stone flight of Keeper's Stairs, increasing her pace as she went. Her initial purpose, her need to search, was swamped by alarm and a desire to escape, for now she had a powerful sense of being followed. It was like the second time she went through the mirror in the Room of Ceremonies, with Davey, when they went after Dr Monckton, the sinister archivist from the city Museum. Then they had been followed by Govan, but she had the definite feeling that this was not him. The sound was different. Govan's feet had pattered, a barefoot boy steps light across the cobbles. This tread was much heavier: a kind of dragging padding. It had started with one set of footsteps, but now there were more . . . Every time she turned, she saw nothing, but as soon as she set off the following started again.

She ran down past the door into the underground city and on to the end of Keeper's Stairs. From there she turned right at the bottom of the steps. She was in a long road curving up and off to the left.

She could not remember ever being in this street before, either waking or dreaming. The whole area seemed to be in a different time again. It was run-down and decaying, but unmistakably modern. Chinese takeaways and Indian restaurants alternated between small shops. Dirt drifted in litter-strewn doorways. The dusty windows stood empty, the glass smashed, or cracked, or boarded up. There was still no one about. She risked a look behind her. She could see nothing, but the presence there was overwhelming. She could hear them coming on. A sharp, high-pitched note echoed above her, to be answered by another. They were whistling, signalling to each other.

Kate ran as fast as she could, chest heaving for breath, heedless now of where she went. This was as real as any waking life she knew. She had lost all sense that she was dreaming.

The road seemed to disappear beneath her feet, turning into a rough track. She was being chased by a whole pack of them. From behind her came the rhythmic rap of pounding feet, sounding almost like hoofbeats. She rounded a corner and found herself on a ledge. On one side the land sloped up, stones and rock topped by rough grass; on the other, a sheer cliff fell away from her. She was on a bluff overlooking the river. The path finished in a dead end. Her pursuers were close behind now. The only way was up.

Small hovels leaned against a cliff face riddled with caves, hollowed-out dwelling places. She looked in, thinking she might be able to hide, but immediately shrank back. Deep inside, white shapes seemed to move and writhe. She skirted the entrances and began to climb. The path took her past a series of crumbling entrances. Soft worm-like things were issuing from them. A clammy hand fastened itself round her ankle, then another, pulling her down . . .

Suddenly there was a man standing above her. He was holding a sword. He slashed left and right. The white shapes shrank back with a whining, mewing noise and a strong arm reached down to pull her up.

'Well, Mistress Kate, you have led us a fine chase.'

It was Jack Cade. Govan was with him. The boy stood panting, hands on thighs.

'The city stripped of ghosts is a dangerous place for mortals to wander in,' the highwayman said, looking about grimly. 'Other things creep out to take their place. Cave wights, banished spectres, all manner of low and evil creatures. The gutter-sweepings of every century . . .' he glanced round warily and did not sheath his sword. 'Come,' he held out his other hand to her, 'we will be safe up here. The Blind Fiddler is waiting. He sensed you searching, both this night and the night before. He sent us to meet you, but we had no way of knowing where you would enter the city. We did not find you until it was almost too late. He is waiting. Come with me . . .'

He took Kate by the hand and led her up to a grassy expanse at the top of the bluff. The turf was short here, springy underfoot. The Blind Fiddler was sitting on an old stone set in the middle of the green sward. He appeared to be staring straight ahead, his long fingers laced round the top of his staff. Elizabeth and Polly sat at his knee, like grandchild and daughter. Govan ran from Jack's side to be with the old man, settling on his other side like a seeing dog.

Opposite the Fiddler's seat stood a high stone wall. It was built right at the edge of the cliff, looking out across the river. It might once have been part of a castle, or some kind of church, but there was nothing now to show what the building had been. All that remained was a ruin, a curtain of stone, fretted with arches and windows.

The ghosts rose in welcome, making room for Kate to join them.

'Welcome, child.' The Blind Fiddler groped for her hand. 'I have been waiting for you. I want to know why you search so diligently, even in your dreams.'

'It's about Davey,' Kate drew nearer. 'I'm worried

about him. He's, he's been so strange lately. It's not just me,' she added, 'Lisa's noticed, too.'

'Lisa?' He asked and Elizabeth looked up at the name of her kin. 'The girl who helped to save him from The Lady?'

'Yes,' Kate nodded. 'We've both seen a big change in him. Ever since Mayday, he's just not been the same.'

'How? How is he changed?'

'He,' Kate paused to think, 'he just doesn't seem to care about anything, or anyone, any more. He spends a lot of time by himself, and at night he wanders about.' Her voice dropped to a whisper as she told him what had happened the night before.

'Hmm, I see.' The Fiddler closed his blind eyes and dropped his head in thought. 'This has happened since Beltane, you say?'

'Beltane?'

'Mayday.'

'Yes. He was quite normal before then.'

The Blind Fiddler beckoned Jack and Elizabeth closer to him. The ghost girl and the highwayman approached from where they had been listening.

'Davey was involved in the episode with the ghost-hunter, was he not?'

Jack nodded.

'Could he have been damaged?'

'I think not,' Jack said.

'He *was* affected by the Cleansing,' Elizabeth added. 'But he seemed to recover from it.'

'I do not think it is that,' Jack shook his head. 'I think it is something else entirely.'

'What?'

'Davey was at the Beltane Fair,' the highwayman looked round cautiously. 'Others were there . . .'

'You mean . . .'

'Yes, They were there, the Fair Folk.' Jack Cade dropped his voice. He disliked even talking about them, let alone using their real names. It was a superstitious dread that went back to his country childhood. 'The Lady and some of her band. I do not know what her intentions were, but you can be sure they were not good. I warned you, Kate, did I not?'

'Yes, and we did lose Davey for a while . . .' Kate paused. 'Do you think she might have got to him? Do you think she might be doing this?'

The Fiddler nodded. 'It is possible. More than possible. The Old Grey Man, her father, has forgiven her Midwinter meddling. She is strong between Beltane and Midsummer, it is her time of year.

Tomorrow is her day, so we must all be very careful . . .'

'But why should she still want Davey so much?'

'Who knows? She sometimes takes a shine to a mortal, man or child, and if she has set her heart on him, she will not be thwarted.'

'Davey wouldn't go with her,' Kate shook her head. 'He hates her.'

'There are many ways . . .' the Fiddler's fingers brushed the strings of the violin he always carried with him. 'I was not always as you see me. Once I was young, and some thought handsome,' his hand strayed to his head and face, 'with thickly curling red hair, a straight nose and lips ever turned up in a smile, and large bright eyes the colour of robins' eggs. I had travelled far from the land of my birth and found myself here at the time of the Beltane Fair. The Fair was a very great gathering, bringing folk from everywhere, both the living and the dead, from this world and others, but I was just a young fiddle player. I knew nothing of that then.

'As I moved through the fair, delighted by the excitement, my eyes feasting on the sights, I heard the most wonderful air, a divine tune, intricate and lyrical, but wild at the same time, played by a master. I followed the sound, seeking to join him and maybe steal from him, for I earned my living by fiddle and bow. I soon found the player, and others too. I joined them, playing alongside them through the night to the day. It was the most dazzling company. The musicians were the finest I had ever heard, and the dancers! One in particular caught my attention. She was the most beautiful girl I had ever seen. She brought me food and she brought me drink; she showered me with gold.' He paused in his telling. 'I stayed with them, as I thought for just a few days, long enough to dally with her, and learn their tunes and take them away. I would be gone by Midsummer.' He gave a laugh, sharp and bitter. 'By then I would be away. I got away all right, and I took with me their tunes, but that was all. For when I left . . .' His hand shook on the neck of the violin. His voice quavered as if at some deep remembered shock, and tears squeezed from his eyes' closed lids. 'When I left, the world was changed and changed again. I was an old man, condemned to wander without sight. She took my eyes because I had seen what I should not.'

'She?' Jack Cade questioned. 'The beautiful girl, she was . . .'

'The Lady?' The Fiddler finished his sentence. 'Indeed, she was. She took my sight, but she made me a seer,' he pointed to his unseeing sockets, 'because that amused her. I could look into men's hearts, but not their faces. I could gaze into the future, but not at the land, or sea or sky. I can still hear her laughing . . .' He shook his white head. 'That is what happens to those to whom The Lady gives her love. She is beautiful beyond words to describe, but cruel beyond the measure of man. She can turn your eyes to wood, your heart to stone. She can come between you, and all that you hold dear, so that all you want is her. I fear that is what she is doing to Davey.'

'What can we do to save him?' Elizabeth had been listening to the tale with mounting horror. She had known something of the Fiddler's story, but not all. 'How can we help him? We must go tomorrow.'

'Kate must bring him here, to the city. We have until the new day dawns to find a way to aid him.'

The Fiddler turned his blind eyes towards the edge of the bluff. The cliff faced east. Across the river, the sky was turning from deep grey-black, becoming lighter, streaked across with long soft ribbons of violet, pink and orange.

'That,' he said, gesturing to the central arch in the wall in front of them. 'That is the Door of No Returning. Tomorrow, as Midsummer dawns, we must pass through.'

45

The tall pointed archway was directly aligned to the rising sun. As Kate watched, the first pinpoint of light broke through the darkness on the far horizon. The rays radiated out into a luminous halo, filling the doorway with dazzling light, spilling across the green to touch the stone on which the Fiddler sat. It seemed that she could see black shadows outlined against the brilliance, as wave after wave of ghosts passed through.

7

Something Wrong with Davey

Kate woke to the clock radio chattering away on the bedside table. She was back in her own room. The duvet was on the floor and the sheet was twisted around her like a rope. The sun was fully up, pouring in through the gap in the curtains. She felt a momentary panic that she'd be late for school, then realised it was Saturday. Normally she loved that feeling; thinking it was a school day and then realising that it was the weekend, but today it held none of the usual pleasure. She sank back against a pillow still damp with tears of fear and nighttime sweat and thought about the dream she'd had. Except it did not seem like a dream. She remembered all of it, for one thing, and she was exhausted. She ached as though she had walked every step.

'Kate?' Her mother's voice came from downstairs. 'Are you up yet? Tom and Ellie will be here any minute.'

Kate looked at the clock. Was that the time? She *had* overslept The twins were going to be dropped off early. Her aunt and uncle were going away for the weekend. Kate got out of bed and stepped into the shower. She stood under the running water, letting it pour over her, trying to wash away her nightmares.

By the time she was dressed and downstairs, the twins were already there, watching TV in the living-room.

'Hi,' she said as she came into the room. 'Here.'

She gave them a present each. Earrings for Ellie, who had just been allowed to have her ears pierced, and a CD for Tom.

'From Davey and me. Happy birthday.'

The Davey part was not strictly true. Kate had bought and wrapped the presents herself. The twins had hit thirteen on Thursday, two days previously, and Davey had forgotten all about it. They wouldn't even have got a card if Mum hadn't sent one for him. As for a present? Forget about it.

'Cool,' the twins said in unison as they unwrapped their presents. 'Thanks.'

'Where's Davey?' Tom asked. Usually his cousin was first down to meet them.

'He's upstairs, I guess.' Kate put out her hand as Tom got up. 'Wait. Before you go to see him, there's something that you ought to know . . .'

Kate turned up the volume on the TV and told them about Davey. She told them about how Lisa had come to her, and the changes they both saw. She told them about seeing his double on the stairs while he was asleep in bed.

'Are you sure it wasn't a dream?' Tom asked.

'I've thought about that,' Kate replied. 'And I'm pretty sure it wasn't. I tell you, Tom, something *really* strange is happening to him.'

'When was this?'

'Night before last.'

'What about the night just gone?'

'This is not to do with Davey, not directly, but I did have the weirdest dream . . .'

'Astral projection.' Elinor remarked when Kate had finished

'I beg your pardon?' Her brother raised a sceptical eyebrow, a look he reserved for when he had not heard of something.

'That's what it's called,' his sister explained with a sigh. 'I saw it on a TV programme. Another name is "lucid dreams", like OBEs—'

'Come again?'

'Out of Body Experiences. People are aware that they are in one place, in bed asleep say, but they

49

appear to be in another place, the ghost city, in this case. Although on one level they know that they are dreaming, the experiences they are having feel totally real to them, not like dreams at all.'

Yes,' Kate said, before Tom could interrupt again. 'That's what it was like exactly.'

'Hmm,' Tom remained unconvinced. 'They could still be just dreams. How would you know for certain that you've had one of these OBEs, or whatever?'

'There's only one way to find out,' Elinor replied. 'We go to the city tonight. Go on the ghost walk as planned. If nothing happens, it was just a dream. If not . . .'

She left the sentence unfinished.

'Yeah, that's a good idea,' Kate agreed.

'What about Davey?' Tom asked.

'What about him?'

'Should he come with us?'

'What do you mean? The Blind Fiddler said—'

'Ah, but if it *was* just a dream, it might be dangerous for him. Taking him into the lion's den, so to speak. It might even be a trap . . .'

'I see what you mean . . .' Kate frowned, suddenly troubled. She hadn't thought about that.

'What if he doesn't want to go anyway?' Elinor

suggested, following her brother's lead. 'It might be better to leave him at home . . .'

'Hmm,' Kate thought for a minute. 'It's been a while since he said anything about it. He might even have forgotten, along with everything else . . .'

'There's one way to find out.' Tom stood up.

'What's that?'

'Ask him what he wants to do. I can stow this at the same time.' Tom picked up his rucksack.

Tom came down, his freckled face pale. His mouth twitched in a slight flinch, and his grey-green eyes were narrowed as if he had recently suffered some kind of blow.

'What's the matter with you?' Elinor asked, alarmed by the obvious pain her twin displayed. 'How's Davey?'

'He – er – invited me to "go away",' Tom replied, trying to smile, trying to make a joke of it. 'Didn't even say "Happy Birthday". One thing you don't have to worry about, though. He won't be going with us tonight. He says he'd rather go to some barbecue.'

'That's where Mum and Dad are going,' Kate explained. 'One of Emma's friend's parents are having a party. We were all invited, but I said we

51

were doing something else. I wouldn't have thought Davey—'

'Whatever.' Tom threw himself down on the settee and concentrated on watching TV. He gradually relaxed, but the hurt expression Ellie saw stayed in place. Although they didn't see each other all the time, Davey and Tom were close – almost like brothers. Davey looked up to Tom, usually they got on really well, so how could Davey treat him like this? She had not yet seen her cousin, but there had to be something very wrong with him. The look on Tom's face convinced her more than anything that Kate could have said.

8

Cave Wights

'Are we going on the Haunts Ghost Tour?' Tom asked as they crossed the bridge into the Old Town.

'No,' Kate shook her head. 'I'm not even sure that they do them any more. Anyway, it would be a waste of time. This isn't a nostalgia trip. We are here to find the ghosts before they leave, to see if they can help Davey.' Kate led them down to the river. 'We'll go this way. It's quicker.'

They picked their way past the clearing and building work still going on as part of the Riverside Development Project. Most of the area was fenced off, but a large part of the old riverbank path was still intact. It wound its way round the old docks and wharves; past warehouses and storehouses that now stood gutted, buildings waiting to be restored and remodelled into flats, offices, a new visitors' centre. The old ships' chandlers' was already undergoing conversion into a maritime museum.

Eventually they ran out of pedestrian pathway

and had to leave the riverside for the streets behind. This was not an area of the city that Tom and Elinor knew at all. The road that they were following seemed pretty run-down, full of tired, dusty shops, shabby-looking pubs and clubs and low-grade cheap hotels.

It led to a long sweeping section of elevated highway that roughly followed the line of the river and formed part of the system of bypasses and link roads looping the city. Two modern bridges joined it on either side of a low bluff.

The bluff was cut off now isolated by the complex of roads designed to keep cars and lorries away from the Old Town. The cliff could only be reached by walking underneath a huge traffic exchange. Kate led them down into a foul-smelling underpass. The tunnel was in need of repair. Pools of unidentified liquid stained the concrete floor. They had to step carefully to avoid pitfalls and places where the yellow graffiti-daubed tiles were flaking off the walls.

The underpass led into a labyrinth of enormous pillars and stanchions that held up the roads circling above. It was dark under there. The far wall was natural rock, the same soft red sandstone Kate had seen last night in her dream. Then the cliff-face had been riddled with caves. They were still there. The hovels were still there, too, although they were now constructed from plastic and cardboard. They were occupied. Kate could see eyes gleaming inside and the glow of a small fire. She looked down at the ground. There were bottles and cans littered around. Kate was reminded of the cave wights, the loathsome cave-dwelling creatures that she had encountered the night before.

A man's voice growled, 'Spare some change,' and she jumped.

'Yeah, any change, pet?' a lighter voice chimed and Kate looked down to see a polystyrene cup thrust towards her, gripped by thick grime-seamed fingers and black and broken nails. Little dark eyes looked out of a mass of matted, straggly hair. A big beard, stained round the mouth, bushed like a cloud of wire wool from underneath a sheeny purple-grey nose.

'How about you? The little ging'er?'

The man next to him leered up at Elinor. He was younger, not much more than a boy. His skin was pale, pimpled and marked by bad nutrition. He took a swig from his beer can and leered again, showing yellow uneven teeth.

Kate was not sure what to do. Tom and Elinor drew nearer to her. All three of them stood staring at the two men until the unmistakable sound of a mobile phone broke into the tense silence growing between them. Kate's hand groped for her pocket. The young man's grin grew wider. Mum had got the phone after the last time they all came back late from the city . . .

'Here you are, mate.' Tom dug into his pocket and threw all the change he had before grabbing Kate, who was staring like a mesmerised rabbit. 'Come on,' he hissed. 'Let's get out of here!'

They ran for stairs that led up to an island surrounded by the whine and drone of traffic. The phone was still trilling. At the top, Tom hung over the steps to see if the men were following. The younger of the two had, indeed, shambled to his feet, but when he saw where they were heading, he hesitated and then went back. Tom leaned back, breathing a sigh of relief that the young tramp could not be bothered to climb all the way up to them.

Kate turned away from the traffic noise to answer the call.

'Sorry,' she said. 'It went off when we were in the middle of the road—

—Do I? We were running—

—Oh, right. Okay, then—

—Er, yes. No. Not right now. He's, he's, um, gone off with Tom somewhere—

'—Yes. Yes. We'll try. See you later. Yes. Bye.'

She folded the phone and put it back in her pocket.

'It's okay,' Tom said to her, jerking his thumb towards the stairs. 'I don't think they can be bothered.' He nodded towards the phone. 'I didn't know you had one of those.'

'Mum bought it after the last time when we all got separated.'

'Was that her?' Elinor asked, alerted by the sick look on Kate's face.

Kate nodded.

'What did she want?'

'She phoned to say that Emma is staying over, so they would be back late.'

'That's all right,' Tom said. 'It gives us more time.'

'That's not all she said.'

'What else?' Elinor came over to her cousin and took her arm. 'Is it about Davey?'

'Yes . . .' Kate bit her lip. 'He's not with them. He's supposed to be, but he's not. She thinks he's with us.'

'And you told her he was with Tom – why didn't you tell her the truth?'

'Because I didn't want to worry her – and it wouldn't make any difference.'

'Try the phone. See if he's at home.'

Kate did as Tom said. There was no reply.

'Where is he?'

Kate sat down on a concrete seat with no back. 'Goodness knows.'

'What are we going to do?'

'Wait here, I suppose.'

Tom and Elinor looked about. The top of the bluff was not much like the vibrant close-cropped green Kate had described from her dream. The wide oval space was choked with car-thrown, wind-blown litter: cans and wrappers, brown paper bags and polystyrene food containers. A few weeds showed here and there, rank yellow flowers, straggling along the path or struggling through long grass, tough and thick, stiff with grey dust and black grit.

'Is this it?' Elinor frowned and Tom looked doubtful.

Kate nodded. This was the right place. The big squat boulder where the Blind Fiddler had been sitting was still there, although almost covered now by a swirling stook of seeding grass. Opposite to it, on the far side, stood the curtain of stone. It looked thinner, more eroded, as frail as lace against the deepening midsummer blue.

'We'll just have to wait,' Kate said. 'Wait for the ghosts to come. They are the only ones who can help us now.'

9

Cat's Cradle

Davey lay on his bed, resting on a cat's cradle of lies. He had never dreamed it would be so simple. First he had told Kate that he did not want to go into the city. He was going with Mum and Dad and Emma to the barbecue party. Kate had not kicked up the kind of fuss he'd thought she would, which was good. She had gone off with Tom and Elinor to get the bus and go on the ghost walk. Then, at the last minute, he'd told Mum and Dad that he'd changed his mind, that he wanted to go to the city after all. He'd left the house, supposedly to follow his sister and cousins, but really he'd doubled back, waited for his parents to leave the house, and then nipped in through the back door.

He had slipped between them. In trying to catch him, they had all missed. He laced his fingers behind his head and stared up at the ceiling with a small smile of satisfaction. Easy.

He lay quietly, watching the changing light from outside slide over the walls. He sought no other amusement. His stereo and TV were silent, the computer screen blank. The games CDs stood neatly stacked, gathering dust. He had no need for them any more. Soon it would be time. Soon.

Downstairs the phone rang and rang, but he took no notice. He kneeled up on the bed, chin on the windowsill, looking out across the tops of the houses to the wild expanse of Wesson Heath. Beyond that, lay the dark green splodges of Kingswood's undulating forest. Haze-filled valleys and tree-serrated ridges stretched ever onwards to the far horizon, suggesting a timeless, mythical landscape, untouched by man's activity. That was where he wanted to be. Away from all human interference. Free and clear.

The dark blue sky was bleeding crimson and orange at the edges, as if lit from below by unseen fires. It seemed that he could see the curvature of the world. Above it all, the midsummer sun hung midway from heaven, falling towards the west like a bloody red ball.

10

Go Well

Elinor was scared. She did not like this place. She was afraid those men might come up after them, but Kate would not hear of going. This was where she had arranged to meet the Blind Fiddler and here she would stay – all night if necessary.

'You can go if you want to,' she said, knowing that they wouldn't leave her.

'But what about those men?'

'They will not come up here, Elinor,' someone said behind her. 'Never fear.' She turned to see the highwayman, Jack Cade. He winked and smiled down at her. 'They think that this place is haunted.'

'Jack!' Kate jumped up. 'Where are the others?'

'They are here.'

She looked around to see Polly and Elizabeth. Standing with them was the Blind Fiddler, his hands resting on Govan's shoulders.

'I didn't hear you.'

Jack's grin widened, and his dark eyes sparkled. 'Of course not. We are ghosts.' He swept off his hat to them all. 'Kate, Tom, Elinor – how do you do? And where is Davey?'

As Kate explained, he became suddenly grave. He listened carefully, not interrupting, turning his hat round in his hands. The others gathered to hear what she was saying. Kate looked from one ghost to the other. They all stared back, their eyes sombre and anxious.

'It is as I feared,' the Fiddler said when she had finished. 'The Lady works to thwart our best endeavours.'

'The Lady?' Elinor looked at him, eyes widening.

'Certainly.'

'But surely, she is nowhere near Davey. I thought that her place was here . . .' Elinor looked out over the bluff, past the circling traffic, towards the Old Town.

'That is just *one* of her places,' the old man corrected her. 'She has many. Another of her places is Dwerry Hollow, as you discovered at Hallowe'en.'

He used the old name: 'Dwerry' meant dwarf, or changeling. Elinor turned away with a shudder, clutching her arms to her. The present evening still held the heat of the day, but she was suddenly wrapped in the freezing temperatures of Derry

House's basement, with the fairy woman's silver eyes staring down into hers.

'So she *could* be at Derry Hollow . . .' Kate said, her mind struggling to take in the implications. 'What about the rest of them? The Host, the Unseelie Court?

The Fiddler shrugged his slightly stooped shoulders. 'All I can say for certain is that they are not here. Their Knowe is empty. I have just come from there. They have either moved to other lodgings or—'

'Or what?' Jack Cade asked, impatiently.

'This year a great Hosting is taking place far to the west. They may have set off for it already, or they may have stopped on their way—'

'To pick up a passenger, as it were.' Tom finished his train of thought.

'Indeed, Thomas.'

'We have to get to him!'

Kate jumped up, frantic. Home. The very place where they thought that Davey would be safe had turned out to hold the greatest danger of all. Derry Hollow was about a hundred metres from their house.

'Wait, Kate! It's no use just racing off. We need to know more before we do that. I don't understand,'

Tom turned to the Blind Fiddler. 'What does she want with Davey, anyway?'

'She is working some deep enchantment, just as she did at midwinter. That time she failed, but she learns from her mistakes. Now she baits her trap with sweetness. She has entered into him, poisoning from within, turning his heart to stone, so he no longer cares for the things of this world. Once the process is complete, it will be impossible to save him. He will be lost forever.'

'How so, Blind Fiddler?' Elizabeth's grey eyes widened with fear for her human friend. 'How so?'

'Before, she sought to capture him. Now he goes of his own free will. Once he is in her power, he will be lost.'

'But how?' Elizabeth's black brows drew together. 'I still do not see . . .'

'Because he will want to stay with her. He will see no reason to return.'

'But what about us?' Kate interjected. 'His family, his friends . . .'

'He will care nothing for you, don't you understand?' The Fiddler shook his head. 'A heart of stone cannot love. He will care nothing for you, or anyone.'

'That—that's awful!' Elinor exclaimed. 'Davey's warm, and considerate. He's—he's generous, and—and affectionate . . .'

Her voice faltered as she took in the enormity of the threat to him. Elinor hated The Lady. Out of everything and everyone that they had encountered since all this started, she feared her most. What she was doing now to Davey was worse than anything Elinor could imagine.

'The enchantment works like their arrows, their elf bolts,' the Fiddler went on. 'If any part remains, the poison will be in him still. He will be *in* this world but not *of* it. He will go through his whole life with a stone where his heart should be . . .'

'You mean he will never love anyone? Ever?'

'That is it exactly.'

'That's—that's terrible. It's evil!'

'Indeed, Elinor,' the Fiddler nodded. 'Indeed it is. You speak more truly than you know.'

'Why are we all standing here *talking*!' Kate exclaimed. 'We've got to find him!' She stared wildly at the circling traffic. 'We ought to get going before it is too late!'

'I'm with you, Mistress Kate,' Jack looked at her. 'Go by any means you may. I will go, too. I can travel more swiftly than you.' He smiled, trying to reassure her. 'I will find him, and I will save him, never fear.'

'And if he is already with The Lady?' Kate asked.

Jack drew his sword. 'She will taste this. Her and her company.'

'No,' the Blind Fiddler flinched at the sound of the blade cutting through the air. 'Your weapon will do more harm than good. Do you not listen? The enchantment must be unwoven, not slashed into pieces.'

'How? How can it be done?'

The Fiddler did not answer straight away. He leaned his clasped hands on the top of his staff and bent his head, turning his sight inwards.

'I cannot see clearly.' He raised his eyes in questing enquiry. 'But you must go and you must take Elizabeth.'

'Why me, Fiddler?' the ghost girl whispered.

'I do not know,' the old man heaved his shoulders, 'I just feel that it is so . . .'

'If I cannot use this,' Jack interrupted, sheathing his sword, 'what am I to do?'

'You will find other ways. Other allies.'

'You speak in riddles, old man,' Jack grimaced. 'You are as bad as *them*.'

'Hush, Jack,' Polly hurried forward. 'He is Davey's only hope. Do as he says.'

'Yes, Jack,' Elizabeth threw her long hair back. 'Why do we delay?'

'Come, then,' Jack held out his gloved hand to her. Dell, his black mare, was tethered below.

'Go well, Jack Cade,' the old man held up his hand in blessing. 'Stay well.'

'You, too. Fiddler. Look after Govan and my Polly.'

'Jack! Elizabeth!' Polly called after them. 'Remember you must be back by first light of dawn!'

Elizabeth nodded to show she understood. Jack just smiled and touched the brim of his hat in a gesture of goodbye. When they had gone, Polly turned her face to hide her sorrow, knowing that she might never see either of them again.

11

The Watcher

Davey stared out of the window watching the great red ball of the sun, split by grey spindrift cloud, stain the whole western sky and sink towards the horizon. Soon it would be time to leave for Derry Hollow.

When only the top of the sun showed like a crimson dome, he stood up and went towards the door as if heeding a distant call.

He left his room without a backward glance. He went down the stairs without turning to see the family photos smiling down at him: grandparents, parents, Davey himself, with Kate, with Emma, all three of them together. He did not as much as glance at the people who meant the most to him, even though he might never see any of them again.

He let himself out of the front door, shutting it carefully behind him, went up the path and turned right into the street. Not once did he look back.

He went on down the road, always downwards, heading for Derry Hollow. The lights were coming on in the houses. TV sets flickered in front rooms;

barbecue smoke wafted over from back gardens. Street toys lay abandoned on drives and lawns, left as their owners went in for the night. Davey strode on, leaving behind the everyday trappings of suburban life.

When he reached Derry Hollow, he stopped. There was no one around. No one was watching him. He took one last look at the place he had lived all his life and followed the sloping ground down towards Derry House.

Davey was wrong. There *was* someone watching. Higher up the hill, on the other side of the Hollow, Lisa was staring out of her bedroom window. She had been watching the sunset, too. Her room was at the top of a block of maisonettes in Garden Court, high up on Puckeridge Rise, and she had a fine view out over Wesson Heath and beyond.

She saw Davey immediately as he came out of Derry Way at the bottom of the cul-de-sac. She watched him stop and gaze around, and wondered where he could be going at this time of night. She looked beyond him, thinking to see Kate and the twins, knowing that they were coming for the weekend, but Davey was alone. There was no sign of anyone else. That did not square with what she knew of Kate's plans. Lisa felt mystery begin to surround his sudden appearance.

Davey did not stay in one place long. He set off down the slope towards Derry House. Lisa got up from her seat, craning for a better look. This was even more unexpected. She did not know exactly what had happened in there last Hallowe'en, but she knew that something had. Davey avoided the place like the plague after that but then, Lisa shivered as goosebumps suddenly furred her arms, didn't everybody?

Now she *knew* there was definitely something strange going on. He was strolling down towards the hulking Victorian house as if he was off to a party.

'I'm just off out, Mum,' she called, grabbing her jacket as she passed the living-room door.

'Where are you going?' Her mum called back.

'See a friend, I won't be long.'

Lisa let herself out through the side door, running down the steps and off down the road into the Hollow.

Derry House driveway was full of skips. She made her way past shards of rotting wood and spilling plaster, walking round the outside of the house. There was no sign of Davey anywhere about.

She went back to her starting point and stopped

for a moment to listen. From somewhere came distant music, but it could have been coming from anywhere on the estate, or even up in the village. The Hollow collected sounds into it, like a natural bowl. Lisa stared up at the house. The doors and the ground-floor windows were boarded. The building had been completely stripped out. You could see sky through the roof beams, joists through the frameless upper-storey windows. Davey could not possibly be inside it. The house had no floors. So where had he gone?

She took one last look at the empty house and headed out on to Wesson Heath.

12

The Old Grey Man

Davey went down into the Hollow, following the drive towards the back of Derry House. As he entered the part in deepest shadow, he saw a man coming towards him. At first, he thought it must be the Blind Fiddler, but though white-haired, this man walked straight, with seeing eyes; he had no need for staff or guide.

'Who are you?' Davey asked, although he already knew the answer.

'You know who I am,' the man's voice had a deep, ringing quality and the words came slowly, as though he was unused to human speech. 'I am the Old Grey Man.'

The leader of the Host. The King of the Unseelie Court. He stood tall, towering over the boy. Davey looked up into a face that was very far from human. His eyes were large, almond-shaped, set wide, stretching almost to the sides of his head. Davey could see no white; pupil and iris were silver. Bones showed clearly beneath skin the colour of pewter.

Great age showed in the fine lines mapping his face and his beard was long. The flowing mass of his hair was the colour and texture of spiders' webs.

'Come,' he offered Davey an impossibly thin, long-fingered hand. 'My daughter is eager to see you. We must not keep her waiting.'

Davey glanced round, suddenly aware of someone else, standing close by the house. As he went towards her, she stepped out.

Davey had always considered The Lady to be beautiful, but now she appeared far, far more than that. She had discarded any pretence of human disguise and was as she is. Her gown was of the finest material, white and shimmering, shot through with silver and gold. Her long fair hair, the colour of ripened wheat, flowed into the folds. Her eyebrows swept up, angled above large, wide, slanting eyes that were the translucent green of emeralds. High cheek-bones and a pointed chin accentuated the hollows in her face. Her wide mouth curved back in a smile, showing small white teeth.

'Welcome, Davey.' She held out her hand to him. Her skin was as smooth as fine white porcelain, absolutely unlined, but her eyes were as deep as the deepest ocean, the expression within them as old as time. 'Welcome to my home. Enter freely.'

74

'Thank you.' Davey stepped towards her, his own eyes circles of pale clear amber. 'Thank you, I will.'

The earth seemed to crack wide for them to go inside. Music floated up from the interior, the most wonderful music Davey had ever heard. The sound mingled with wild high cries, the excited calls he remembered from the Mayday Fair. Davey quickened his step. It meant *those* people were there. The Lady put her arm around his shoulder as she led him down the gentle slope and into the fairy knowe.

'They are all waiting for you. It is your home now.'

Davey went gladly. This seemed so right. It felt as though he had been waiting for this moment since before the beginning of his life. Over his head, The Lady smiled at her father. The Old Grey Man smiled back at her. He did not understand why she had set her heart on this human boy, but she was his beloved daughter, he could deny her nothing. The Old Grey Man looked down at the child walking between them. As soon as the earth closed behind them, this boy would forget that he had ever known any other life.

13

Return Journey

Jack Cade rode with Elizabeth, taking Harrow Lane down to the river. From here he took the footbridge across to what remained of the old roads: back streets and twisting cobbled alleys; parts of dual carriageway; footpaths through bleak industrial estates and high-rise housing developments. He went through the city's outskirts and into suburbs that once had been ploughland, woodland, fields and meadows. All along the way stood stones, old posts and crosses, some lost, some removed, some still there but weed-choked and long-neglected, placed to mark the old track that led to Wesson Heath.

No one saw him, but a few people shivered and looked up to see if the sun was clouding. Here and there, dogs barked. Cats bristled, hissing at nothing. Horses shied, scattering from their grazing as he passed by.

Nothing could impede a ghost horse and riders. They made good progress. Better progress than Kate,

Tom and Elinor. They left Polly with the Blind Fiddler and Govan and slogged their way through underpasses and overpasses up to the new road interchange. From there they took one of the new motorway bridges across the river.

The wide road did not make pleasant walking. Three lanes of cars and lorries streamed in either direction. The noise was constant. Dust made their eyes sore and gritty; their throats and noses felt choked, blocked with exhaust fumes.

Once they were over the river, Kate found the right bus stop, but they had to wait for what seemed like ages for a bus to come along. Then, when they were on, it seemed to stop at every possible stop. Kate scowled at the slow snake of passengers shuffling on and off and stared out of the window in an agony of impatience.

'I've known speedier *snails*,' Tom whispered as the bus lumbered and juddered through the traffic.

The streets were full, the pavements crowded. The warm June evening had brought everybody out. Time was getting on. Neon showed from cafés and restaurants. Light spilled from pubs and late-opening shops.

'Come on! Come on!' Kate sat forward in her seat, urging the bus on, just as she had done as a small child.

'What are we going to do when we get there?' Elinor asked. 'See if he's at your house?'

'No,' Kate grimaced. 'There's no point. He's not going to be sitting there waiting for us, is he?'

'Where will he be, then?'

'I don't know. It's up to us to find him.'

'But how can we? Perhaps we'd better go and find Auntie Alison and Uncle Stephen . . .'

'And tell them what?' Kate turned on her cousin, blue eyes blazing. 'It's gone too far for that. They wouldn't listen to us, you know what adults are like. They might *say* Davey's away with the fairies, but I don't think though know how close to the truth that is. They might even call the police, and would *they* listen? It would just mean a massive big fuss and we *still* wouldn't get him back.'

Elinor wasn't sure. She looked at her brother.

'What do you think, Tom?'

'I'm with Kate. We've got to do this on our own and hope we can get to him before anyone realises that he is missing.'

'How do we do that?'

'I don't know,' her brother shrugged. 'Wait for inspiration to strike, I suppose. I wish Davey was here . . .' he added and then grinned at what he'd said. 'Well, he *is* the one who has feelings and intuitions—'

'And if we're going to find him, we're going to have to think like him. You're a genius, Tom! Come on,' Kate stood up and reached for the buzzer above her head.

'But we're not there yet!'

'I know, but Wesson Heath's the next stop.'

'I don't recognise it.'

Elinor looked out of the window, frowning. The bus was speeding up, the stops were getting less frequent. The road they were on crossed a little patch of country, a gap between the suburbs, a green space that had yet to be erased.

'Me neither,' Tom agreed. 'I thought it wasn't for ages.'

'This is Wesson Heath Common, not the village.' Kate stood poised as the bus doors wheezed open. 'And this is where we are getting off.'

14

Wesson Heath

The evening was still warm. Lisa tied her jacket round her waist and followed the same route that Davey had taken at Hallowe'en: across the field, over Gilmore Bridge, along Shaker's Lane and on to Wesson Heath.

Shaker's Lane sloped down into the Hollow Road; a road so old it seemed to have been worn down into the land. Heathland rose up on either side, unfenced, uncultivated. There were no neat hedges here, only patches of gorse and scrub. The few trees were gnarled and bent. Lisa came to a twisted old oak, dwarfed by the wind. Here the way forked. One path led to a green way, unnamed and unpaved, an ancient foot-trodden path passing through a shallow valley and on to the westward expanse of Wesson Heath. The Heath had once covered a much bigger area, spreading wild and open for many miles, before merging into the King's Wood, which had been part of a great forest extending far to the west and south.

The other road led up to Whitestone Hill, the

highest point on the Heath. Lisa followed this route, almost without thinking. Even though it was a fine evening, she didn't see any people about. No one came here much, except in the winter to toboggan or for Sunday afternoon rambles, or to walk their dogs. At the top of the hill, this road met three others. The crossroads made a good vantage point. An excellent place to look out for Davey. The summit was marked by the Whitestone, a dirty quartz boulder that lay beside the four roads. Lisa stood on this, shading her eyes.

The setting sun struck across the heath, kindling the gorse to fire, bathing everything in a strange red light. Lisa squinted hard but the glare made it difficult to see a thing.

There was no sign of Davey. It was as if he had vanished into the ground. She got down from the Whitestone and sat on it, chin resting on her hands, wondering what to do.

Far across the heath, Jack's sharp eyes caught the shape of a child sitting on the stone.

'There! Over there!'

He turned Dell's head and made for the White-stone. At Hallowe'en he'd found Davey waiting at the crossroads.

Elizabeth looked out from behind him, peering over his shoulder. As Dell drew nearer, she could see that the child was a girl, not a boy. Although they were dressed in similar ways, in short-sleeved jersey shirt and coarse blue cotton trousers, the figure was slighter, the hair longer and much curlier.

'It's not him,' she said to Jack.

Jack reined Dell in, set to wheel her back to the path that would take them to Derry Hollow.

'Wait,' Elizabeth gripped his shoulder. 'It is his friend, Lisa. The child who saved him at Midwinter. She is kin to me . . .' Elizabeth paused. 'I sense a certain symmetry. What did the Fiddler say? You will find other allies, other ways? She may have a part to play.'

'There is sense in what you say.' Jack thought it over. 'And we have no other ideas. Night draws on.' The sky above was turning an ever-deeper blue and over towards the west it was a mass of red. He spurred his horse on. 'Let us see if you are right.'

15

The Search

Tom and Elinor followed Kate up on to Wesson Heath, although they were both sure that they had got off at the wrong stop.

The sun was going down, slanting red rays across the rough country, making it hard to see anything. Different paths snaked away in different directions. They were not sure where they were going, so did not know which one to take. On a map, the area looked small, but they were on foot, without even a bike between them. They were also tired from their tramp through the city. Wesson Heath spread out all around them and seemed vast.

'Which way?' Tom asked.

Kate shook he head. None of them was blessed with Davey's sixth sense. Now they were up here, the guiding intuition, which had said to get off the bus, seemed to have tuned itself out.

Tom looked around, eyeing the rising ground.

'Let's make for the middle,' he pointed up towards Whitestone Hill. 'From up there, we can see where we are. We can have a good look round as we go, and then, if we don't find anything, we can make for home.'

'We ought to look in Derry Hollow . . .' Elinor added, although this was the last place she felt like going.

'Yes,' Tom agreed. 'We should. Come on, then. Time's wasting.'

The distance did not seem so far, once they had an objective in view. Kate was all for setting off across country, but Tom said that was not a good idea. It might *seem* the quickest way, but the ground in between might be rougher than it looked, with hidden dips, impassable scrub and boggy places. So they stuck to the old road that still traversed the common. It was much easier to walk on its metalled surface, even if it was full of potholes and the unkerbed verges were eroded and broken.

The road undulated over the countryside. Tom looked up as they reached the last rise. The cross-roads seemed to be occupied.

Lisa started with surprise. She had been so far into her thoughts and dreams she might as well have been asleep. She had heard nothing. No sound had roused her, no hoofbeats drumming on the road, coming nearer and nearer. She sensed, rather than knew, that someone, or something, was suddenly there, standing right behind her. Her grey eyes widened and her heart jumped up into her throat as she turned and looked up into the froth-flecked, blood-rimmed nostrils of an enormous horse.

The animal stood huge above her. It tossed its head, sweat showing on the rippled muscles of its great black neck. This could not be happening. Lisa closed her eyes and opened them again. She must still be dreaming. The horse was bad enough, but between its twitching ears she could see a highwayman looking down at her, complete with mask and velvet jacket.

Her first instinct was to run, but her legs seemed to have frozen under her. All she could do was stare.

'It's all right, Lisa,' a voice said at her side. 'Don't be alarmed. Do you remember me?'

Lisa nodded. It was Elizabeth Hamilton, the ghost of her great-great-aunt. In looks they were almost identical. The same grey eyes, set wide in a heart-shaped face. The same strong black brows meeting above a straight slightly snubbed nose, and the same full mouth above a chin with a slight cleft.

'Don't be afraid of Jack,' Elizabeth said, and the highwayman smiled and swept off his hat. 'Or Dell.'

The horse neighed at the sound of her name and tossed her black mane. 'They are friends of Davey. We are worried about him, just as I know you are, and we've come here to look for him.'

'Me, too.'

'How so?' Elizabeth's brows drew together in enquiry.

'I thought he was going with Kate and his cousins into town, but then I saw him going down into the Hollow, into the grounds of Derry House.' Lisa shrugged. 'I wondered what he was doing, so I followed him.'

'But he wasn't there?'

'No,' she shrugged again and spread her hands. 'It was as if the earth had swallowed him up . . .'

'You speak more truthfully than you know . . .' the highwayman remarked gloomily. He had dismounted now and was standing beside her, his arms folded.

'Shh,' Elizabeth scowled at him. 'Quiet, Jack! Go on, Lisa.'

'There's not much more to tell. I thought he might have come up here, so I wandered up to have a look but there's no sign of him.'

'Hmm.' Jack took a moment to consider, his chin resting on his gloved fist. 'And you have seen nothing since you came up here? Nothing, shall we say, unusual?'

'No,' Lisa shook her head. 'Nothing at all. The place seems quite deserted.'

'Or heard anything?'

'No . . .' Lisa shook her head again. 'Although – wait a minute! I *did* hear something. Kind of distant music . . .'

'What kind of music?'

'Old-fashioned, but not classical. You know, with fiddles and flutes, kind of folk or Irish, something like that.'

'Where did you hear this?' Jack asked.

'Down in Derry Hollow.'

Jack looked at Elizabeth who nodded. 'That sounds like them,' she said.

'Like who?'

'Do you remember The Lady?'

Lisa nodded, thinking of the creature who had taken the shape of Miss Malkin. Lisa had never seen The Lady, except as the teacher, but had experienced the power she could wield; warping time, twisting fate. Just before Christmas she had done just that, nearly destroying Davey and Lisa herself.

'Well,' Elizabeth looked at her. They appeared to be about the same age, but the girl standing here was her great-grand-niece. 'We think that she has taken Davey and this time she means to keep him.'

'But how? Davey would never stay. He will try to escape, put up a fight—'

'Not this time,' Elizabeth shook her head. 'The Lady is subtle, full of cunning and cleverness. She learns from her mistakes. She seems to have worked some kind of enchantment, so he goes to her willingly. She has been preparing him. She must have got to him at some point without anyone realising and planted the spell like poison in his mind. Now he *wants* to be one of them, which makes everything much more difficult than if she had taken him by force.'

'Them? You mean there's more . . .'

'Oh, yes. Scores. Hundreds very probably. They are the Sidhe. The Unseelie Court.'

'And Davey wants to be with them?'

'So it seems.'

It sounded as if The Lady had kind of brainwashed him. Of course! That would account for his strange behaviour. Lisa suddenly understood.

'He hasn't been the same since he went to that fair at Mayday,' she said. 'He came back raving about some ride he'd been on, and the people he'd met. The way he went on about them, I thought he'd met a pop star or something . . .'

'That was when it must have happened. I warned Kate that they were about . . .' Jack Cade's face darkened with anger, more at himself than anybody else. He pounded one gloved hand into the palm of the other.

'It's no good blaming yourself, Jack,' Elizabeth laid a hand on his arm. 'We just have to decide what to do now.'

'We can't take the Hollow. We would not even be able to get in. We have not the magic. The Old Grey Man will be there in person. Even the Fiddler would not gain entry without his permission.'

'So what do we do?'

'Wait for them to come out.' Jack looked out over Wesson Heath. 'Tonight is Midsummer. They will ride. The Fiddler said they are hosting far to the west. They will not leave it much after sunset. We can guess the route they will take.'

'How?' Lisa asked.

'Their horses are unshod. They will keep to the old green ways and grass roads and they will be heading west to the setting sun. We will lie in wait. The best place will be where two ways cross. I know just the spot. The whole Host will be there. All the Unseelie Court. They will come by in a long cavalcade led by the Old Grey Man and his daughter.

Davey will probably be just behind them. When he rides by, we will seize him.'

'What if we don't manage it?' Lisa's grey eyes narrowed. It seemed like a tall order to her.

'If we do not, they will enter the King's Wood. It will be much more difficult for us to take him once he enters there.'

'So what if we can't do that, either?'

'After the King's Wood, the Host will take to the air. If that happens Davey will be lost forever. You will never see him again.'

16

The Host Rides Out

Jack knew Wesson Heath like he knew his own hand. He led them down one bumpy furze-lined track, and on to another. Every now and then, he lifted his head to scan the horizon. Once or twice he whistled through his white teeth, a single sharp and piercing note.

'What do you look for?' Elizabeth asked. 'The Unseelie Court?'

'No,' Jack gave a grim smile. 'They will not come yet.'

'Who do you call?'

'One who might be of assistance. What did the Fiddler say? You will find other allies, other ways?' He quoted her words back to her. 'Thank you for reminding me, Elizabeth.'

They came to a point where four paths met. Another twisted tree grew here, an old thorn with no leaves and the branches bent up, like fingers clawing the sky. A huge patch of brambles tangled around it, almost covering a crumbling stump of stone that stood at its base. This was all that remained of the Mile Cross, an ancient signpost that marked the meeting of ancient boundaries, and a parting of the ways. To the south lay the village. To the north lay more open heathland. East was the way they had come. A broad green path led west, wide enough to take horsemen riding four abreast. That way led into the dark forest depths and was all set around with ferns. The turf there was soft and springy, velvet as a lawn.

'This is the place!' Jack tethered Dell to the thorn and pointed to the patch of bramble and briar. 'Hide yourselves!'

'How long do we have to wait?' Lisa whispered, briar thorns grabbing at her arms, tangling in her hair.

Lisa slipped her jacket on. The sun had gone from the west and, although it was a warm night, a chill white mist was sneaking up the sunken road from the south, spreading out like thin gauze.

'Not long, I think, Ssh,' Jack put a finger to his lips. 'Do you hear it?

Lisa listened. At first she heard nothing, then came the ching, ching, chinking ring of many small bells, followed by the soft thud and pad of unshod hooves. The rhythmic ring and silvery jingle jangle of bridle bells was accompanied by wild high laughter that did not sound human. Strange, eerie cries echoed, like birds calling to each other in the gathering darkness. The Fairy Court was abroad.

Lisa knew what they were but, until now, her imagination had furnished their appearance. Her eyes widened in awe as she saw the beings, who were winding their way up the path towards her. These were nothing like the creatures she had created in her mind from films and toys and fairy tales.

They were as tall as humans, slenderly built, pale in the half light, with high cheekbones and slanting eyes. Their long hair flowed as they rode, glowing like burning sheaves of silver and gold. Lisa caught her breath and held it. They were beautiful!

Two columns came towards her, riding one after another. The first were clad in grey, mounted on black horses. Short-bladed swords hung from the riders' belts. Some had quivers of arrows and small deeply curved bows slung across their shoulders. Others carried long lances tipped by silver leaf-shaped blades.

Behind his guard came the Old Grey Man, grey-haired, grey-bearded, grey-gowned, wearing a simple silver crown. He was riding a fine steed, dappled like dull beaten steel, richly caparisoned in silk and lace as fine as cobwebs.

The following troop rode on chestnut bays. Their clothes were paler, silver-bright, and they seemed younger, wilder, laughing and joking with each other, enjoying the cavalcade. They were armed, as before, with lance, bow and sword.

This was The Lady's own guard, her personal band. Behind them she came, riding on a horse of dazzling whiteness, her silver bridle trailing silk. She looked very young, and very beautiful, as she joked with those nearest to her, shaking her silver hair so it streamed behind her, glittering like moonlight on a river. She was smiling and laughing, her slanting eyes gleaming green beneath a pale circlet of gold. Her long gown draped down, flowing in folds, shimmering to matched the shifting change in her eyes, from silver to green and back again.

Behind her came another milk-white steed, smaller than hers, little bigger than a pony. On it rode Davey. But how he was changed! Lisa gasped, her eyes wide with wonder. He had become one of them! He was dressed like the rest in grey and silver. His features had taken on a fine chiselled cast and his eyes gleamed pale amber. His dark hair clung to his head, sleek as fur, and a gold star shone on his brow.

The Lady turned to gaze back at him, her silver eyes gleaming with pride and hard-won possession.

Then the column broke. The first group, with her in it, wheeled to take the curving turn in the road that would lead them to the west. Their bridle bells jingled, and their pace increased to a canter as soon as their steeds' unshod hooves touched the springy surface of the velvet turf.

Two red lights blinked and shone from the ridge opposite. Above the riding column, the Guytrash watched and waited. The huge black dog had been tracking the Fairy Raid, keeping pace with them across the heath. This was his place. He had no quarrel with the Old Grey Man, but he had no love for The Lady, or any of her band. The Guytrash was a wily and canny hunter. He kept his great red eyes firmly on his quarry, the human child. He tensed now, judging the moment, his body taut and ready, his huge strength coiled back into his massive haunches. When the column split, he pounced.

17

Red Lights

Kate sat on the Whitestone. Tom said he'd seen figures up here on the hill. He'd thought it looked like a man on a horse, which could have been Jack. He'd thought he saw others close beside him, smaller, more childlike in size. One of them could have been Elizabeth. And the other? It could have been Davey. Kate had needed no more prompting. She'd run up and down the hills, forcing her way through gorse and briar and bracken. Her clothes were torn, she was covered in scratches, but when they got here, it had all been for nothing. There was no sign of anybody.

She wiped her eyes, smearing tears of bitter disappointment across the dirt on her face.

'People don't just disappear,' Elinor was saying. 'We ought to go back. Maybe he just went to bed, or something—'

'And maybe he didn't,' Kate glared up at her. 'And people *do* disappear. Don't you ever read the papers? Hundreds of them every year.'

'Yeah, but they aren't usually taken by fairies. There are rational explanations—'

'Oh, really? You've *seen* her, Ellie. She'd have taken that other little boy last year. He would have been a goner if Davey hadn't saved him.' Kate turned away as fresh tears started. 'Oh, how I wish, how I *wish* that we'd *listened* to him. He didn't want to go, remember?' Kate closed her eyes recalling last midsummer. 'If we'd listened to him, we never would have gone on that stupid ghost walk!'

'Yes, well, we did, didn't we?' Tom scuffed the grit at the side of the crossroads. 'There's no point in crying over it, and there's no point taking it out on Ellie. She's only trying to help.'

'I know,' Kate sniffed and wiped her nose on her sleeve. 'Sorry.'

'That's okay. Here—' Elinor offered her a tissue.

'Thanks.'

'That's okay,' Elinor shrugged, hands in pockets. 'You keep it. I don't want it back.'

'What's that?' Something, a glint in the distance, had caught Tom's eye. He stood out in the crossroads, shading his eyes, gazing out to the west.

'What's what?'

'Over there,' Tom pointed. 'A red light. There it is again.'

Kate peered into the gathering darkness. 'Perhaps it's the sun, reflecting on something.'

'The sun's gone. Set.'

'Perhaps it's a car,' Elinor suggested.

'With red headlights?'

'Rear lights, then. You know, brake lights—'

Kate shook her head. 'There aren't any roads over there.' She looked around. 'Everything looks different somehow, the Heath looks bigger . . . Perhaps it's a UFO,' she managed a lopsided grin. 'Seriously! There have been sightings out here. It's a whatd'ya-callit? Hot spot. Or maybe it's those other things, earth lights—'

'Red lights, earth lights, UFO – whatever it is, it's weird,' Tom stared intensely. 'And weird is what we're looking for. Come on, let's go and see.'

18

Away

The white pony whinnied, rolling its eyes in terror, as the huge dog leapt straight for it. It shied, rearing on its hind legs. Davey lost his grip on the reins and fell backwards out of the saddle. The Guytrash was on him in the blink of an eye. The huge creature seized him in his massive jaws and began to drag him away from the milling confusion and up on to the opposite bank.

Fairy lances whistled past his gigantic head. A dart embedded itself in his shaggy neck. The Guytrash dropped his burden and turned, growling. Davey lay pale and crumpled between the paws of the great creature. Lisa thought he must be dead. The Guytrash moved forward, ready to meet his attackers, careful to put his enormous body between Davey and them. Lisa acted instinctively, without thought. In a second, she was out of her hiding-place, sprinting across the space in between. She knelt over Davey, feeling for his pulse, touching his face to see if he was still alive. His eyes were closed and he felt so cold. She took her green jacket off to cover him and put her arms round him to keep him warm.

'Lisa!' Elizabeth rose to go after her, but Jack held her back.

'Wait! We should not intervene.'

'How do you know?'

'I feel it is so. The Guytrash will not allow any harm to come to her. Perhaps it is meant.'

Elizabeth looked at the scene in front of her and whispered, 'I certainly hope you are right.'

The Guytrash was completely surrounded. His red eyes blazed and he continued to snarl his defiance. His tormentors danced out of the way of his scything paws and snapping jaws, jabbing at him with their leaf-bladed lances. They were aiming at his eyes, trying to blind him, while ranks of bowmen advanced upon him, short bows drawn to their deepest extent, ready to discharge their bolts deep into his flesh.

One word and he would be stuck like a pincushion. The Lady was standing in her stirrups, her emerald eyes, sparking cold fury, urging them on to the kill.

Suddenly a deep voice rang out like a bell.

'Hold!' The Old Grey Man ordered the circling warriors, his hand held high in command. 'I will not have the Old One harmed!' He pointed towards where the Guytrash stood at bay. The massive animal looked up, his huge lamp-like eyes glowing bright in recognition. 'He walked these hills before ever we came here.' The Old Grey Man twisted in his saddle to face his daughter. 'This thing has gone on too long. I say, enough! The choice has been made.' He pointed to where Davey lay, cradled in Lisa's arms. 'The Old One has saved the human child. One of his own has claimed him to herself.' He turned back to his daughter. 'You must meddle no further. They have him fast.' The Lady stared over at the human boy whom she had coveted for so long. Her emerald eyes flared defiance, and her band looked to her, weapons drawn in readiness. Then she lowered her gaze. The Old Grey Man was both her father and her king. She was bound to him by blood and sealty – bonds that even one dare not break. 'It is settled then, daughter,' the Old Grey Man said, inclining his head, accepting her obedience. 'We will tarry here no longer. We have far to go this night. Come,' he wheeled his steed and pointed westward. 'We must away!'

The lancers and bowmen lowered their weapons and returned to their horses. The leading rider lifted a great green horn from his side and blew. A series of powerful notes belled through the gathering darkness. The Old Grey Man's call was taken in a general shout: 'Away! Away!'

The Old Grey Man spurred his horse and the whole column galloped after him headlong down the broad green path, and then they seemed to rise up, blackening the sky, blotting out the stars and the rising moon. The air was full of their wild high cries as they wheeled and turned, streaming off into the west like a great flock of migrating birds.

19

Stay Well

'They are gone.' Jack said, as he stepped from his hiding-place. 'You are safe. They will not return.'

Lisa looked up at him, her grey eyes all pupil. It was only now that she was beginning to realise exactly what she had done. Before it had been like a dream. Now she was waking up to find herself in the middle of the Heath, with a highwayman bending over her and Davey lying limp and still, half in her arms, half in her lap. She looked from him to the great shaggy bulk of the Guytrash sprawled close by and her eyes widened still further.

'Don't be alarmed,' Jack squeezed her shoulder. 'He will not harm you. See? He has pains of his own to deal with.'

The Guytrash was whining now, and licking himself, searching for hurts in his fur like any other dog.

'Come, Sir,' Jack addressed him formally. 'Let me look at you.'

The huge creature looked up, his red eyes

dimmed by the wounds he had received. His enormous tongue unfurled from between long white teeth as sharp as knives and he licked Jack's hand. Then he shuffled over, awkwardly, on forelegs and haunches and licked Davey's face, as if his hot rough tongue could lick the life back into him.

It seemed to work. Under the rasping tongue, some of Davey's colour began to come back. He stirred and struggled, muttering to himself, as if in sleep. He was becoming too much for Lisa to hold. Elizabeth helped her to sit him up and between them they held him as he twisted and turned, wriggled and squirmed, became very hot and then very cold. Lisa wrapped her coat round him tighter. His eyes moved under the lids, his lips shaped words and he made sounds, although no sounds they could understand. It was as if he was vividly dreaming, and in the dream he was transforming, changing from one shape into another.

All they could do was hold him. Jack looked at him closely, peeling his eyelid back. The eyeball moved, scanning some inner world that only he could see.

'At least he's still alive, and not with *them*,' Jack said.

'Will he come out of it?' Lisa asked.

'I don't know. Keep him warm. Hold him tight. While I tend to the Guytrash.'

Jack searched through the twisted cables of the creature's thick fur, looking for elf bolts, the short-shafted lethal darts that the Fair Folk had discharged. The Guytrash lay obedient, head on paws, hardly flinching. Only the odd twitch of the skin or lift of the head showed the pain he was suffering. Jack lined the arrows up in a row. Luckily none of them had penetrated very deeply. Most of the wounds were superficial. The important thing was to get them all out. They were cunningly made. He turned one between finger and thumb, admiring the elegant feathered flights and finely knapped razor-sharp blades. They were set about with spells besides. Any left beneath the skin would cause the flesh to fester, and might even work their way deep inside and through to his heart. He looked at the white streak left by an old wound in the big dog's black flank. This was the second time that he had saved the Guytrash.

When he had finished, Jack wiped his hands on the grass and came to see how Davey was doing.

'He's quieter now,' Lisa said. 'But he shows no signs of coming out of it.' She bit her lip. 'Perhaps we should get him to a doctor . . .'

Jack laughed out loud. 'Leeches have no cure for what ails this boy. Lay him next to the Guytrash. They can warm each other.'

Lisa was not sure, but she did as she was told. The great dog turned his head, the light showing red from under the lids. He nosed Davey as though the boy was a puppy and began to lick him again. The big tongue was warm and wet, and as rough as sandpaper. This time Davey did more than stir. He put his hand up to his face.

'Ugh! Get off me!' He opened his eyes to see what it was, his features twisted in a grimace of disgust.

'Davey!' Lisa put her arms round him, hugging him to her.

'You can get off, too,' Davey struggled to escape her embrace, thinking it was Kate. Then his deep brown eyes widened as he saw who it was. 'Lisa? What are you doing? What is the matter with you?'

She held his chin, looking deep into his eyes.

'They're brown! They're brown! Oh, Davey!' She grinned at him. 'I could kiss you!'

'Well, don't,' Davey edged away. 'Of course they're brown. What colour do you think they'd be?' He edged away a bit farther, in case Lisa had turned into a crazy person.

'It's all right, Davey.' Elizabeth smiled down at him. 'We're not insane. Just glad to have you back.'

'Where have I been?' Davey looked around. 'What am I doing here? What's been happening?'

'It's a long story—'

'Is that Jack? And the Guytrash?' The great dog was lumbering to its feet. 'Is that what licked me?' Davey put his hand to his face again. 'No wonder it felt like I was trapped in a car wash.'

Davey really was back. His eyes were their normal deep brown. He sat up, Lisa's jacket falling from him. Even the strange shimmering clothes he'd worn had changed back to the jeans and T-shirt he'd been wearing when he left the house. He looked around. They were on the Heath somewhere, he could work that much out, but why, and how he had got there, he had no idea.

The Guytrash stood up slowly, staggering slightly, then shook himself, the movement rippling from nose to tail, like a dog shaking off water. He moved his big head from side to side, looking from one to the other, then he raised his nose, as though he had caught another scent in the air, something new and interesting. It was time for him to go. He gave a whine, as if in farewell. Jack bowed and wished him goodnight. He knew better than to thank him for his help.

'We must leave, too,' he said after the Guytrash had gone. 'We must return to the city or Polly will worry. At dawn we depart. We must be back long before that.'

'Depart?' Davey looked up, puzzled and concerned. 'Where to? Where are you going?'

'We are leaving the city. All the ghosts.'

'Polly and Govan? The Fiddler, too?'

'All.'

'Forever?'

'Yes,' Jack said quietly, bowing his head.

Oh, no . . .' Davey said.

Jack, Elizabeth, Polly, Govan and the Fiddler might be ghosts, but they were his friends. At the thought of losing them, of never ever seeing them again, Davey's heart seemed to swell painfully in his chest. It was like the feeling rushing back into a limb after some extended paralysis. First came pins and needles, then shooting agonising pain. Davey winced and his eyes filled. He sat where he was. The feeling was so intense it was physical.

'It is time for us to go,' Elizabeth knelt down beside him, putting her arm round him. 'Thanks to you, the Judge and the Sentinels rule no longer. The Book of Possibilities is closed. What Was, and What Is, have become What *Has* to Be.'

'I understand, I do,' Davey blinked the tears back. 'It's just . . .'

'Do you not think we feel the same way, too?' Elizabeth squeezed his shoulder. 'We will miss you, but we must leave now. We must. To everything there is a time, and our time has come.'

'I know,' Davey sniffed. It was like coming home from a bitter wind-blown frozen wilderness only to find that all your friends were leaving.

'We will meet again. Some day you, too, will go through the Door of No Returning.'

'Where does it lead?'

'To the other side.'

'What is it like?'

'We don't know,' Elizabeth stared away into the darkness. 'No one ever comes back. One day you will find out.' Her mouth curled in a smile, but her eyes stayed sad. 'But not for a good long while I hope.'

Davey looked at her and saw a girl who was younger than he was now. Their eyes met, and hers seemed suddenly full of tears, but whether she cried for him, or for what might have been, he just couldn't tell.

'Ghosts don't cry,' she said, smiling again as Davey took a handkerchief from his pocket.

'Elizabeth,' Jack was calling her. 'Time runs on.'

'I must go,' she reached over and kissed him lightly. Her lips felt cool and soft on his cheek.

'Go safely, Elizabeth,' he whispered.

'Stay well, Davey.'

20

The Way Home

Jack did not like goodbyes.

'Come, Elizabeth. We have far to travel,' he said, helping her up into the saddle. 'And you,' he turned to Davey, his dark handsome face serious and sad for a moment. Then he smiled and his black eyes gleamed with unexpected tenderness. He tapped the boy gently on the side of his face, two gloved fingers tipping his chin. 'You stay away from trouble.'

Then he was mounted. He saluted once from the back of his horse, waving his hat in farewell, and he was gone. Davey sank back to the ground buried his head in his hands, and cried.

'Never mind, Davey, never mind,' Lisa said, putting her arm round him. 'It's probably for the best. They *have* to go. You heard what they said.'

'I know, it's just . . .' Davey's muffled voice came back.

'Have a good cry,' she patted his back. 'Does you good sometimes, that's what my gran says.'

Especially after what happened to you, she thought, but she didn't tell him that. His tears were cleansing, healing, washing away the poison inside him, replacing it with human feeling.

'We'd better think about getting back ourselves,' she said, after he seemed to have cried himself out. 'Mum will be wondering where I am.'

She didn't want to alarm anybody, but that was probably a bit of an understatement. It was a wonder search and rescue helicopters weren't circling right this second.

'Can you walk okay?' she asked as she helped him to his feet.

'Yeah, I'll be fine,' he leaned on her shoulder. 'Just give me a minute.'

They had been sitting down in between thickets of bracken and gorse. As soon as they stood up, they became visible. They rose, almost at Tom's feet, as unexpected as a couple of pheasant. He jumped back in surprise from where he'd been standing, staring around, wondering where else to look. The source of his red lights had long ago melted away into the night.

'Hey, Ellie, Kate, over here!' Tom shouted, waving to his sister and cousin. 'Where did you two spring from?'

'Nowhere. We've been here all the time . . .'

'We've been looking everywhere. Are you all right?' He looked at Davey. 'Kate's been ever so worried.'

'Yeah, I'm okay,' Davey started to say, but just then Kate came running over.

'Lisa! What are you doing here? Are you all right?' She turned to her brother. Her intense relief at finding him again melting into concern at the shake in his voice, the whiteness of his face. She began looking in his eyes like a doctor.

'I'm fine, Kate,' Davey struggled out of her grip. 'Get off me!'

'He seems okay,' Lisa intervened. She was afraid that Kate's fretting might be too much for Davey's newly-hatched feelings. 'Has anyone got a watch?' She asked, deliberately changing the subject. 'I left mine at home, but I think it's late.' She looked at Tom's wrist and went pale. 'I'd better go. My mum'll kill me.'

'Here,' Kate handed her the mobile phone. 'Ring her on this. Say you're at our house.'

'But it's only just round the corner,' Lisa punched in the number. 'She'll want me back – like – now.'

'Say you're staying over.'

'Thanks, Kate. That's a great idea.'

*　　*　　*

113

As soon as Lisa finished her call, the phone rang. It was Alison Williams wanting to know why there was no one at home.

'Hi, Mum.' Kate replied. 'We're round at Lisa's house—

—Lisa Wilson, Davey's friend—

—All of us. Yeah. Playing a game—

—Kind of a war thing, involving fairies and elves and stuff—

—Soon, yeah. I *know* she *only lives* round the corner—

—Okay, okay. Oh, Mum – can Lisa stay the night—?

—Well, because . . .

—I know, but she wants to—

—She can sleep in Emma's room—

—Great! Thanks, Mum!

—Yeah. See you later.

'That's all sorted then.' Kate returned the phone to her inside pocket. 'Let's go home.'

It was strange. Each of them thought the village was a long, long way from this place on the Heath, and that it would take them ages to reach it. But that wasn't the case. In what seemed like no time, they were in amongst familiar surroundings, walking on the pavement of their own estate. They all knew that time could shift, and with it space, so perhaps Wesson Heath itself had changed, shrinking back from a wild expanse to its present day, more user-friendly size. Either that, or maybe the way back is always shorter, an easier distance to make than the outward journey into places unknown.

21

The Door of No Returning

They travelled quickly, the way it is in dreams. One second you are in one place, the next you are in quite another. Davey, Kate, Tom, Elinor and Lisa. They looked at each other and knew that they were dreaming the same thing, at the same time, which was an impossible thing. They were dreaming all together.

They were in a high place looking out over the river. They were here to see their friends. They were here to say goodbye.

At the very edge of the cliff stood the high wall, the curtain of stone, fretted like lace with arches and windows. The central archway was tall and pointed like an arrow head. This was the Door of No Returning The time was midsummer dawning. It was time for the ghosts to pass through.

Their friends were there and waiting for them. Jack and Polly stood together, their hands loosely linked. Elizabeth and Govan stood either side of the Blind Fiddler, who no longer carried a staff, his hands resting on their shoulders. The children approached, their dream tread as silent as a ghost walking. Their friends heard them, and smiled in greeting, but their eyes were already fixed on the far horizon.

The cliff faced east. Across the river, the sky was beginning to lighten from indigo to deep cobalt. As the children watched, the first point of light pricked the dark intense blue. Rays radiated out into a luminous halo, filling the Door of No Returning, turning the short springy grass to vibrant greenness, touching the big squat boulder in the centre, making it taller, thinner, casting a shadow like a finger pointing straight towards them.

The Door of No Returning spilled whiteness. The time for leaving was fast approaching. Wave after wave of black shapes showed against the blazing light. On the very brink of departure, their ghost friends turned to smile again and even the dawn's brilliance could not match the radiance on their faces. There could be no more sadness, all sense of sorrow was wiped away.

Davey was convinced of the rightness of things, as one by one, the ghosts left, passing like shadows, to be lost in the dazzling brightness of the sun's new day.

H.A.U.N.T.S

By Celia Rees

Books 1: H is for Haunting

Day and night, all through the city, ghosts of the past shadow the present – some are deadly, others mean no harm. Few mortals can slip into their world, but those who do must fight to stay alive . . .

It is Midsummer's Eve, just before dusk. Davey, Kate, Elinor and Tom embark on the city's Ghost Tour – an unforgettable journey back and forth in time, crossing an unknown and terrifying threshold.

Look out for more books in this series . . .

H.A.U.N.T.S

By Celia Rees

Books 2: *A is for Apparition*

Day and night, all through the city, ghosts of the past shadow the present – some are deadly, others mean no harm. Few mortals can slip into their world, but those who do must fight to stay alive . . .

It is Hallowe'en night, and Davey, Kate, Elinor and Tom go trick-or-treating. But not all the ghosts and phantoms that roam the streets are harmless. Some are truly the living dead . . .

Look out for more books in this series . . .

H.A.U.N.T.S

By Celia Rees

Books 3: U is for Unbeliever

Day and night, all through the city, ghosts of the past shadow the present – some are deadly, others mean no harm. Few mortals can slip into their world, but those who do must fight to stay alive . . .

It is just before Christmas and Davey receives a warning from a trusted friend . . . A ghostly enemy is out to get him. He must stay away from the city centre or be caught forever in a deadly time trap . . .

Look out for more books in this series . . .

H.A.U.N.T.S

By Celia Rees

Books 4: N is for Nightmare

Day and night, all through the city, ghosts of the past shadow the present – some are deadly, others mean no harm. Few mortals can slip into their world, but those who do must fight to stay alive . . .

When ancient bones are discovered on an archaeological dig, powerful, unearthly forces are unleashed. Davey, Kate, Elinor and Tom are caught up in a ghostly battle for these sacred relics, and now they face the wrath of deadly vengeful spirits . . .

Look out for more books in this series . . .

H.A.U.N.T.S

All Hodder Children's books are available at your local bookshop or newsagent, or can be ordered direct from the publisher. Just tick the titles you want and fill in the form below. Prices and availability subject to change without notice.

Hodder Children's Books, Cash Sales Departmnt, Bookpoint, 39 Milton Park, Abingdon, OXON, OX14 4TD, UK. If you have a credit card you may order by telephone – (01253) 400414.

Please enclose a cheque or postal order made payable to Bookpoint Ltd to the value of the cover price and allow the following for postage and packing:
UK & BFPO – £1.00 for the first book, 50p for the second book, and 30p for each additional book ordered up to a maximum charge of £3.00.
OVERSEAS & EIRE – £2.00 for the first book, £1.00 for the second book, and 50p for each additional book.

Name ....
....
Address..
....

If you would prefer to pay by credit card, please complete:
Please debit my Visa/Access/Diner's Card/American Express (delete as applicable) card no:

Signature ....
Expiry Date ....